HWG

HAZEL WOOD GIRL

JUDY MAY

THE O'BRIEN PRESS
DUBLIN

First published 2007 by The O'Brien Press Ltd,
12 Terenure Road East, Rathgar, Dublin 6, Ireland.
Tel: +353 1 4923333; Fax: +353 1 4922777
E-mail: books@obrien.ie
Website: www.obrien.ie

ISBN: 978-0-86278-992-3

British Library Cataloguing in Publication Data
May, Judy
Hazel Wood girl. - (Journal series)
1. Teenage girls - Fiction 2. Young adult fiction
I. Title
823.9'2[J]

1 2 3 4 5 6 7 8 9 10
07 08 09 10 11 12 13 14

The O'Brien Press
receives assistance from

Printed and bound in the UK by J.H. Haynes & Co Ltd, Sparkford

To Audrey Doherty, aka Bangles,
for all we've enjoyed together.

I have NO friends

DAY ONE

I have NO friends. None. Count them.

It's OFFICIAL since last night, and I can't even feel angry any more these days. I don't feel anything now, it's like having pins-and-needles in the places where I used to feel happy or sad. I mean, God, you'd think that I could make *one person* like me after six months here. I can't believe people are still pissed off that I had lunch with Danny from chemistry when I didn't even *know* he'd been that girl's boyfriend for the last million years. I think they just like having someone easy to hate. Possible Solution: I need a brother, or even another sister to hang out with, and maybe then *I'd* get to be the ignorer for a change. And I could tell them things and they'd have to behind her. Or a parrot! That would do the job, and I could go all super-geek and teach it to say,

'Poppy girl, you are the best person ever in the whole history of everything!'

Only except Mindy would sneak up to it at night, and re-train it to worship *her*.

OK, BRING IT ON! Chapter one million of the moan-fest! Why not? Even my old friends from the city haven't called or written back in forever, so I have to write in this or I'll go properly, grown-up mental and start talking to the sheep AND (as if we needed further proof of my defectiveness) it's not like this notebook is some wonderful pink and silver job like Mindy has with butterflies in the corners, but I think I ripped out most of the bits that had old homework notes.

I bet I could go the whole summer without talking to one single person.

LIST OF POSSIBLES FOR ME TO TALK TO:
Mum (way too efficient)
Dad (way too jokey)
Mindy (away for weeks)
Trug the sheepdog (limited conversationalist)
Dad's Cousin Adam who lives with us (too weird)

Adam is OK, but not exactly what you'd call normal, what with the way he talks so loud like he's always standing in traffic and the way he doesn't eat or wear anything not officially, by-the-book, organic and ethical. Super-weird for a farmer. I hope he doesn't wonder why he can't get a girlfriend.

Tonight I am going to iron my hair to make it go straight (my hair-straighteners are another thing that got lost in the move), and put in lemon so it will go from light brown to blonde. If I look better, then they might forget that I don't talk the same or have the right clothes. What worked in the city doesn't look good here for some weird reason. I was hoping that writing in this would make me feel better, but I now actually feel *worse*, which I didn't think was possible. Last night's COMPLETE DISASTER was something that belonged on a sit-com end-of-series special, and has me doomed to cringe every fifteen minutes until the end of time itself.

The main reason it hurts is because I really made a *huge* effort, and thought it would be amazing and I'd finally have friends. Mum should have *told* me that they wear jeans and stuff to dances here, after all, she did grow up in the countryside. And that way I wouldn't have turned up looking like a Christmas catalogue compared to the rest of them. An hour can feel like a year; one hour exactly, standing at the side of the badly-decorated school hall in my *stupid* short, red dress and high heels and no one even said 'hello' back when I said 'hello'! After that I just waited in the ladies' toilets until Adam collected me. I was there for ages in the end stall, hoping no one would guess it was the same person in there all the time. At one point I heard my favourite song playing and couldn't even go out for that. *Mortification* with a capital 'M'. I think I will just stay in my room until I am seventy when half the people from last night will have lost their minds or be dead. And I am NEVER wearing that red dress again.

DAY TWO

More grief. Much more! I am only writing in this hoping it will stop me feeling sick every time I think about it. It's like a nightmare or something that should be happening to someone else. In school for the last few weeks they've been talking about 'The Farmer', asking, 'Is The Farmer coming?' or, 'Have you *seen* what The Farmer is wearing today?' I've been wondering who The Farmer is, but was too shy to ask anyone. Then today just before geography class, I worked out that it's <u>ME</u>. God, they *so* hate me!

I felt so stupid and so *nothing* that I ran home right after geography without telling anyone, and hid in my room until the time I usually get back, when I crept out and came back in through the kitchen all noisy and clattering about. Since then I've just been lying on my bed, going over and over it all in my head. The Farmer.

The Farmer! Why can't they find another torture-victim and just leave me alone for once?

I just keep imagining we're back in our old home. I know Dad was sick of the accounting thing, but I'm still in shock and amazement that he got Mum to stop lawyering. I think they saw a reality show about leaving the luxury of the city and living off the land, and bought into the whole hype.

And as if I needed even *more* hassle (I mean, why stop until I'm friendless, homeless *and* hairless?), I burned my hair a bit last night and it still stayed curly, especially because I had to wash it again because the lemon was so sticky and made me smell like a pancake.

I keep pretending I'm OK, but really I feel like I will break. Will they stop if I break?

I bet some of them have never even been to the city and still they call *me* 'The Farmer'. I tried telling Mum and she said not to take them seriously or they'll win. I tried to tell her that they already have won, but she was busy matching socks. Even socks are more important than me.

LATER

I asked Dad can I join Mindy at the French summer school and he said 'no' and something about maturity. She is only two years older than me and she went two years ago so it's not fair. Nothing's fair. It's all Mum and Dad's fault for moving us. They don't even care that they have ruined *everything*.

TREES TREES TREES TREES TREES TREES TREES TREES TREES TREES TREES

DAY THREE

Dad is immersed in his book on trees again and says that the long double line of trees that are on the way to school is made up of elm trees. I would never admit to liking anything around here, but I do love how the double line of them makes a sort of roof, like a grand palace. When I walk under it I pretend I'm a magical, royal creature of the woods. I know that's stupid and like I'm seven or something, but it's the only way I can stand going to school.

Today I ate breakfast during the walk, because the breakfast table was unbearable again with everyone talking about the farm and the problems, and Dad eating half a pig's worth of bacon over his notes, and Mum pretending to have a headache so Adam will leave her alone about the non-organicness of the coffee.

I can fit two slices of peanut-butter toast into my pocket, made into a sandwich so it doesn't go mushy all over the lining. Today I pretended it was doused in a mystical power-giving potion that would make me say and do all the right things, and then finished it quickly before I got to the main road so no one would see. I was reminded it was really only peanut butter when that massive girl with the loud voice and blue eyeliner tripped me up on my way in the gate. I didn't even get my mandarin orange back because it rolled under a teacher's car.

They are having a field day now that Mindy's not around to even pretend to care.

Only three days to go.

DAY FOUR

We had a free class because the English teacher said that we could use the time to get to be better communicators. It was SO obvious that it was because she couldn't be bothered teaching us anything new and because she wanted to read her book. (It's the sort of book that would never get on the curriculum from the look of the muscley man on the cover.) So we had to talk to someone in the class we didn't really know and find out about them and their family and what they liked doing. I looked at Barbara Montague because I always thought she might want to be my friend once she knew me, or at least not ignore me, but everyone just talked to their mates and Miss Phillips didn't notice that I sat there all class just watching people talking. I did try to say something to Matthew Blondel, but he just looked embarrassed and moved away, and it's not like he's the most popular guy in school.

In exactly 1,192 days I will be eighteen. Then I will move to Paris and become wonderful, and get re-married every two-and-a-half years to richer and richer men, and live in bigger and bigger houses until I wind up in the palace at Versailles. I will be a sculptor and a musician and a writer, and have more friends even than shoes, and that will be hundreds. Please let that be true, please don't let me be here on my own while Mindy has a life.

'hello'

hell

'hello'

'hello'

DAY FIVE

Today was a good day. I walked slower than normal so I didn't get to the school road for ages and Barbara Montague was dropped off at the crossroads at the same time. I said 'hello' because I am an idiot and still always say 'hello' even when people blank me, but today she asked me what I was doing for the summer holidays. I was so floored that I couldn't think of anything and so I said,

'Not much.'

Then she told me all about how her family was going to an island off the west coast of Africa and how they had horses and dirt bikes and a swimming pool there. I think she just asked me about my summer so she could show off about hers, but I'd want to tell everyone if I was going somewhere fantastic, so I understood. It's the first time in ages that I had someone to walk into school with, even if she did dump me for a group of girls in the year above as soon as we got near the cloakrooms. It's an OK start.

Mindy always speeds up whenever we get to the gate so she can talk to guys she likes without her sister there getting in the way.

I told Mum and Dad about Barbara and her holiday and Mum suggested maybe she'd let me go with them for a couple of weeks, and so I know she really doesn't get that I don't have any friends. She thinks it's like before when I had loads of friends in my old school. I wish I could go back and maybe live with one of them.

It is MENTAL

It is MENTAL

DAY SIX

I nearly *died* today, and I'm so glad that it was the last day of term. I am too furious even to cry. I still can't believe it. It is MENTAL. Mum went behind my back last night and phoned Barbara's mum (who she sees at yoga) to suggest that I go with them to the island to keep Barbara company. Then her mum went and asked Barbara who said 'no way', that she didn't even know me. And then Barbara's mum lied to my mum and said that she already had a friend going and that there wasn't enough room for anyone else.

And then it was all around the school, which is how I know the whole story, and people were pretending to ask me on holiday with them and laughing. Also, no one told me that you are allowed to wear your own clothes on the last day of term so I was the only one wearing school uniform.

The good news is that it can't get any worse. And the bad news is ... that it can't get any worse.

I didn't want to go back along the main road after school in case I bumped into Barbara, so I went the long way home by the library and took out this home-study kit for learning French. In our class we don't start French until next year and I really need to get going sooner than that, I might get rescued and whisked off to Paris any day now (yeah, as *if*). I wish I thought of it before, I could have been listening to the audio stuff on the walk to-and-from school. Mindy always listens to music when she walks with me and sometimes she gets to borrow Mum's bike and cycles on ahead of me, so it's not like I was crazy-busy doing anything else.

Going the long way round meant I had to pass the Egg Farm. Of course Mr and Mrs Granger were there, and of course they yelled at me, screaming,

'What are you doing on our land?'

But I wasn't, I was just on the edge of the road. Weird because they've met me before when Dad took us around for an introduction, but they were nasty then too. I think that's why they work with chickens, because they can't work with people. They are like storybook baddies, with him all heavy and red-faced, and her stick-thin and wringing her hands together that way. Except they don't have 'redeeming features', which book-baddies always seem to have. They're fairly hilarious, not that you'd ever dare laugh or they might, I don't know, set a pack of rabid chickens after you.

Anyway I was so depressed that even they couldn't make me feel any worse. I am giving up and will just go and lie in a field until someone scrapes me up and sends me somewhere.

LAMBS LAMBS LAMBS LAMBS LAMBS LAM
LAMBS LAMBS LAMBS LAMBS LAMBS LAM
LAMBS LAMBS LAMBS LAMBS LAMBS
MBS LAMBS LAMBS LAMBS LAMBS
LAMBS LAMBS LAMBS
LAMBS

DAY SEVEN

Dad took the lambs away today and put them back
in the sheep field, although you couldn't really call
them lambs any more. They get boring once they're
big, so I wasn't bothered. It's funny how me and
Mindy sometimes do get along, like when we would
tie a string around the lambs' necks and walk them
like little dogs and get them to jump over fences and
things. But that was weeks ago, and now they are
like sheep and only eat. Even giving them bottles
became a pain when we had to do it three times a
day. I do like looking at all the cows and sheep in the
fields, but you get used to that too. It's not all that
thrilling living on a farm, not like I thought it would
be when they first told us. I think I will ask Dad can I

have something new and original like a snake or a chinchilla or a duck, just to see his reaction, but he will probably say it's too dangerous. I wonder how mature he'll say you have to be to own a duck.

I just sat on my bed all day listening to the French course, learning basic phrases. If I land in Paris tomorrow I will be fine for fruit tarts and hotel rooms.

***

I wish someone would ask me how I am.

woodlice & earwigs

DAY EIGHT

I brought a blanket into the greenhouse and some stuff to kill the woodlice and earwigs. It is now not nearly as bad as it was before. Then, because there is nothing else on the planet for me to do, I fixed the broken bit of glass with a wooden tray from the kitchen, which I have never seen anyone use. One really good bit is the way I can see the summer cattle-field from the greenhouse. I must find a chair to bring in.

During lunch (one more meal a day to suffer through now that it's the holidays) Adam said that two little boys and their mother are moving in to the house at the far side of the summer cattle-field. I bet they find this greenhouse and wreck it with stones.

Adam said I could spend the summer babysitting for their mother who isn't well, and he even said it like it was a good idea, which is part of his mental-ness.

That made Mum ask me what I wanted to do for the summer and I didn't dare open my mouth in case she got busy organising, so I said

'I don't know.'

I say that a lot.

Then, even though I was eating in a way that made it obvious that I didn't want a conversation, she said what a pity Barbara already had a friend going with her to the island. Mum really super-size doesn't get it. I think the coffee wrecked her brain a long time ago. She bought me something unwearable in town, and I said thank you and did a pretty good pretend smile.

I worked out that most days I say about fifty words out loud (but always in a nice, polite voice, not sulky or looking for attention – Mum and Dad really stamp down on 'tone'). When you include 'pass the milk please', and 'sorry' and all the 'I don't know's, that's not a lot of things said. There's a gazillion words inside me, they just seem to get stuck on the wrong side of my mouth. I get scared that I will make people angry or make them not like me, unless I pretend to be OK and say OK things.

DAY NINE

My cousin Jen phoned and said she will not be coming over this summer so now there is only Paris in four years to look forward to. In town with Mum earlier I waited for her outside the post-office and saw that friend of Barbara's who is not in our school, who I think is called Emma-Jo. A few months ago I saw them and their mothers together in the café, and Barbara gabs on and on about how her friend Emma-Jo is going to be famous some day. So I'm adding one-and-one together and getting this blonde girl.

She walks like a cat or a film star, and has very short fair hair and the greenest green eyes. I wish my eyes were a real colour like blue or green or brown and not just the colour of beer, as Adam so kindly puts it. Dad tried to make me feel better by correcting Adam and saying my eyes were in fact the colour of barley, but beer is made from barley so he just confirmed it really.

DAY TEN

Breakfast is made more bearable by Mum's new passion for baking muffins. She thinks it makes her creative, but it doesn't, it just proves she can tell a blueberry from a banana. Dad let slip that Adam is going out on a date with some teacher from our school. I hope she dumps him quickly so he doesn't get round to talking about me. Adam is ancient in every way, so either the teacher is desperate, or is Miss Abingdale (forty-ish maths teacher) or both. Dad thinks it's hilarious and Mum thinks it's sweet, and I think it's a bit sick. For God's sake, he doesn't even eat most supermarket or restaurant food without asking loads of questions. Where will he take her to dinner? The carrot and parsnip furrow in our kitchen garden maybe?

I must make something happen. Life is not made up of muffins and sheep. Or at least, it shouldn't be.

Now that I know how to dress in French, and tell the time in French (as long as it is something past something and not something to something), I feel more than ready to leave the farm. Twitchy, even.

I phoned Michelle to see if I could come and visit. It's weird seeing someone every day since you were four and then just not seeing them again. Her dad answered and told me she was away at ballet camp, which I knew but forgot.

My next plan was to phone Mindy and get her to casually ask Mum and Dad to let me join her at French summer camp, and hope that they were feeling unnaturally optimistic at that moment. But she said she didn't want the extra responsibility of having to look after me. She is *such* a pain, she has never had to look after me, even when we were little I always took care of myself. She thinks because she is two years older than me that she's a million times better than me. Only her hair and boyfriends make her a bit better than me, the rest is about even. I didn't argue with her because I never do because there's no point.

Plan C was to eat, and that was successful

because it didn't require anyone being not at ballet camp, or being not annoying. There was some butternut squash soup and I took a mug of it out to my greenhouse to write this.

Just now I saw one of the new little boys from the house across the way, standing stock-still in the summer cattle field. He looks about eight years old and has really black hair and dark-brown eyes. He doesn't seem like someone who would wreck your greenhouse on you, in fact I felt a bit bad for him, just standing there staring into space. I remember how I did that when we first moved. Like if I stood there long enough it would all disappear and go back to being the old place.

DAY ELEVEN

I saw the strange little boy again this morning. He just stands there, gazing out with those big brown eyes, like he's sleepwalking or something. I think it was the same little boy, but it might have been his brother. If I see him again I might say hello.

Adam is smiling *way* too much. Not happy about that, and still no more clues. It might even be Miss Jenkins in which case I might have got Adam all wrong.

Today I decided I would be an intrepid adventurer and fully explore the farm, all around the edge of it. It doesn't take much to be intrepid around here, just way too much time and a bottle of orange juice in your pocket and maybe a banana muffin. I was careful not to go by the big stone barn because that's right beside the Egg Farm and I didn't fancy the Grangers having a go at me again.

I always thought there was nothing but roughland between the sheep field and the falling-down cottage, but in that bit where it dips and curves around the corner, there's a little wood-type place in the hollow. There's only about forty little trees, which are really huge big bushes I guess. They are hazel trees, and it's meant to be called a coppice. I found out when I got back and looked it up in Dad's tree book. I am still going to call it a wood because it is one really. I like the idea of having my own magic Hazel Wood.

Adam said that if I had found the hazel coppice in the spring I would have seen all the lambs' tails hanging there, which are like furry bits that hang off the ends of the twigs. Not real lambs' tails obviously, because that would be more than a big bit weird. He told me they used to use the wood from hazel to make fencing and baskets when he was little. I pretended to be surprised that baskets had already been invented back then.

Today wasn't even worth writing about.

I hope I am not getting ruined for life by all this.

DAY TWELVE

It was hot today so I had my peanut-butter toast-sandwich and blueberry muffin outside, sitting on the drystone wall beside the Hazel Wood and the old, ruined cottage. I don't know why I like it there so much, I suppose because it's sort of off-to-the-side and ignored, and I can relate.

I spent the whole morning there, daydreaming about having a boyfriend and walking past Barbara with my boyfriend's arm around me (and the rest of him attached to his arm, obviously).

Whenever I feel really alone, I always imagine JL, the boy from my old class in the city. In the real world JL is probably spending the summer at the youth club like last year. He used to play table tennis with Mindy and her best friend. If I'd had any clue then that I'd be leaving in six months I would have definitely talked to him, definitely.

Someone I did talk to today was the little boy who was in our farmyard. Well, I said 'hello' and he sort of stared more. What is wrong with everybody that no one can say hello to me? Anyway, Mum says that his mother is sick and that their dad left them when the youngest son was born, so it's got to be tough.

They call him Sammy-boy (sounds like an old American cowboy name!) and his brother is Christophe, but Christophe must be even shyer because I haven't even seen him about at all.

DAY THIRTEEN

Mum sent me over to the new lady's house with a welcome gift of oatcakes, goose eggs and fruit and things, while she went to yoga.

I figured as long as they weren't as nasty as the Grangers I'd be fine.

The Hoopers (that's their name) have been so creative with the house and it looks like something you'd see in an expensive magazine. Mrs Hooper is really gentle and interesting and doesn't look sick, but Mum says that's because it's a condition that comes and goes, worse some days and better others. She invited me to drop in any time and hang out with Sammy-boy and Christophe. I don't want to be rude, but I'm certain that hanging out with a fourteen-year-old girl would be last thing on earth eight- and ten-year-old boys would want.

On the way back through the summer cattle-field one of the cows tried to butt me, so I called it a Sunday Roast and told it where to go. I thought I heard someone laughing, but maybe I am just a bit paranoid after all that's been going on.

I then did something that is so stupid that the word 'stupid' doesn't even cover it. I found JL's number from directory inquiries and called his house. He answered and I hung up. I would so not be good as a spy.

By that stage I was determined to do something positive. Anything to not have it be another wasted day. I read somewhere that rinsing your hair in beer makes it shiny, so I took a bottle from the fridge and Dad caught me going upstairs with it and now he and Mum want to have a chat with me. It's funny really, I'm probably the last person to drink beer and now I have to have a heavy full-on conversation. It's typical, I never do anything wrong and things always go bad.

Something good has to happen soon. Has to.

Broccoli Broccoli Broccoli Broccoli Broccoli Broccoli Broccoli Broccoli

DAY FOURTEEN

Broccoli does not by rights belong in a muffin. You would think that would be obvious.

I think they believe me about the beer being for my hair, but I'm not certain. Still they told me that it's a very busy time, their first year at the farm, and they need me to keep out of trouble.

I was in a full-on strop after that, but I smiled and didn't let them see. I'm sick to death of being nice no matter what, so I stayed away all day, with a serious amount of cheese crackers in one pocket and some grapes in the other.

I headed straight for the Hazel Wood and it was so weird, there was this note hanging from one of the branches of the first big tree. It said 'To the Hazel Wood Girl', and I wanted so badly to have a look inside, but was afraid that the Hazel Wood Girl would catch me at it and be angry, so I just left it and went back to ....

OH MY GOD! I am such an idiot. It might be for me! There are no other girls around now that Mindy's away and we own the wood, so it must mean me. I'm big-time ridiculous, I'm so slow, just like when they called me 'The Farmer', only this is better if it is me. It's only just getting dark so I'm going to run out and see if it's still there. Why am I still here writing this? Oh my God!!!

It was still there!! It says,

Please don't be so sad, Hazel Wood Girl, there are lots of good things around you. Your mission (should you choose to accept it) is to 1) find the newest animal in the farmyard 2) find the strangest-looking creature on the farm 3) find one thing that reminds you most of when you were really happy.

I'd think Mrs Hooper left it, except that from the handwriting it seems to be from a teenager. It's no one's handwriting from our house and it can't be the

Grangers on the Egg Farm because they are biologically incapable of being nice or interesting, and if they did send a note it would be to yell at you on paper.

I just showed the envelope to Mum and she said that seeing as it was in our bit of woodland that it must be for me and that we know everyone in the area so it must be a friend of the family. Of course she thinks it's Barbara, not knowing that she's left already. I'm glad Mum wasn't that interested as it still feels like my own secret. I'm psyched now about getting up and finding out those bits of info asked in the note. It's not the most thrilling thing to do when you compare it to what Mindy and Barbara are up to, but hey, at least it's something.

DAY FIFTEEN

All morning I snooped round the farmyard and the farm (getting under people's feet apparently, even if they were yards away). By lunchtime I was sure of the answers and ran down to the Hazel Wood. My note read,

1) The newest animal is a black calf that was born a month ago. I think there might also be some baby mice in the tool shed in the kitchen garden because I heard tiny, tiny squeaking, but couldn't see them. 2) The strangest-looking creature on the farm is dad's Cousin Adam, no contest. 3) I haven't found anything that reminds me of when I was happy because anything we brought with us makes me feel sad. Sorry if I failed the last part of the mission.

I left it on the tree where I found the original and put

'To The Watcher' on the envelope, as I guess they must have been watching me hang out in the wood. I have been forcing myself not to go back and look again until tomorrow.

Adam was getting dressed up all fancy again (which for him means no welly-boots) so I just asked him,

'Which teacher are you going out with?'

He said, 'Liza' as he walked out the door, which is no help at all seeing as I don't know any of the teachers' first names.

Mum is annoyed because the geese are not laying so many eggs this week. Dad pissed her off more when he said he'd have a word with them about it. Then he made her a coffee and she calmed down. I wish my life was that easily fixed.

DAY SIXTEEN

I saw Barbara's ridiculously beautiful friend Emma-Jo in town again today.

She was talking to this cute guy with dark eyes and dark hair who is *really* tall and a bit gangly, like he hasn't quite grown into himself, and wears a leather jacket and nods a lot when he listens. He has this *amazing* smile, which I know sounds like a cliché, but he really does. Emma-Jo was so into him, talking his ear off about God knows what. I'm just jealous that it was *her* talking to a guy, and that she could think of things to say. I would have just stood there like a lemon. Which reminds me, I put the lemon in my hair yesterday and it has sort of worked a bit, but not so as you'd notice.

Dad said we had to get rid of the rabbit as it ate all the carrots in the kitchen garden. I told him we didn't have a rabbit and he was all surprised. Dads are not good about pets, ages, clothes, birthdays or friends' names. I suggested that maybe Adam was giving bunches of carrots to his new girlfriend instead of bunches of flowers.

I found out that it's Miss Dobbs the supply teacher he's seeing, so it's almost like she's not really a teacher at my school because she was only there for two weeks this term, and then was at other schools further away when their versions of Mr Hackett the history teacher got their versions of ulcerated hernias.

I have been writing this to stop myself running down to the Hazel Wood in case there is no note for me and I'll be all disappointed like some starving puppy with a rubber bone. But now if I wait any longer I will rupture my head, so I *have* to go see.

***

Cool, brilliant and excellent, and not necessarily in that order. There was a note and it said that I carried out the mission *admirably*. I like that. My new task is 1) make something for someone, 2) have a conversation with someone new, 3) fix something I have broken.

I am going to make a welcome card for Mrs Hooper, talk to little Sammy-boy (who is now hanging out around the farm every day), and maybe fix the handle back on the mug I broke when I tried to make gravy in it on Mum's birthday.

I called JL again and hung up again. One more time and I'm on track for a criminal record.

DAY SEVENTEEN

Drawing's not my thing, but Mrs Hooper loved her welcome-to-the neighbourhood card. Sammy-boy was actually there in the kitchen with his mum so I had a quick chat, where I just asked him a bunch of questions and he said yes or no or mumbled. That took care of the 'conversation with someone new' bit of it.

I fixed the mug too, but I don't really think that's what the note meant. So I phoned Mindy and asked her did she want me to look after anything of hers while she was away, like water her plant or wash some clothes. She was really surprised and said 'no thanks', and then she had to go kayaking. But I know I wasn't very nice to her the last time we spoke, so now I feel like I fixed that. I will now write it all up and run down to the Hazel Wood.

SMILEY SMILEY :-)

DAY EIGHTEEN

On the way back through the town from fetching the cattle-feed in the jeep with Dad, I saw that tall, smiley, dark-haired guy again, this time on his own. I know he doesn't go to our school so maybe he is just here visiting relatives for a week. Hopefully he has nothing to do with the Grangers on the Egg Farm. Even driving past the Egg Farm makes me feel like I've caught something; it's so manky, with rubbish everywhere. The poor hens must be miserable!

Going with Dad meant I didn't get to the Hazel

Wood until the afternoon, which was good because I wasn't hanging out for it like a spare.

Today's note from The Watcher reads,

Great job, Hazel Wood Girl.

Today's mission is as follows: 1) Tell me a joke 2) Who do you think I am? 3) Do something outrageous.

From,

The Watcher

OK, I can tell the joke about 'What's brown and sticky? – A stick', because it's the only one I can ever remember. I'm thinking now that maybe Dad is The Watcher, but I'm not certain. I know Dad would only be trying to cheer me up, but that would be a major downer. No, I have a strong feeling it's someone more on my wavelength, an actual friend.

As for the 'outrageous' thing, I'm not exactly the outrageous kind. The worst I've ever done is say that I don't like cheesecake when it's supposed to be everyone's favourite. Or maybe bunking off school that day I found out that they call me The Farmer.

Anyway it says, 'Do something outrageous,' which

means something new.

Mrs Hooper came around to our house tonight and was talking away to Mum in the kitchen for ages. Mum said,

'Of course, you've met Poppy, our quiet one.'

They both said I should go around and keep Christophe company. Yeah, like I'd be up for playing computer games and talking about skateboards or whatever little boys are into. That's the worst thing about living out here, your choice of people to hang out with is very limited. Especially when none of the hopefuls will look your way. I am going to write a letter to JL just for the hell of it and to stop me phoning.

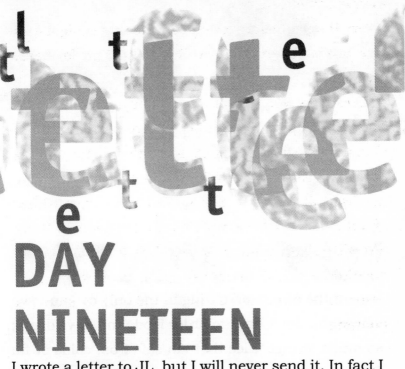

DAY NINETEEN

I wrote a letter to JL, but I will never send it. In fact I burned it already in the bathroom sink and the burning smell stuck around. Now Mum and Dad think I am smoking and we have to have another conversation tonight.

I asked Adam did he know any jokes and he said none that my Dad would forgive him for telling me. So, I guess it's the sticky stick joke then. Can't think of anything outrageous to do.

DAY TWENTY

I spent the afternoon sitting in the only café in town where you don't have to order food, and have drunk so much orange juice that I'm safe from colds or flu for the next ten years.

I really miss my old café in the city beside the art gallery, the one that changed its name and menu every six months. And the way I could go to see a movie, or shop, or all those basic things, every day if I wanted. Now even getting a decent haircut involves a military-style plan and three week's notice. What's the point of living far away from the things that you need to have a life?

I have been daydreaming about JL so much that it doesn't even feel good any more. Like when you sit in a hot bath for too long and go all wrinkly, you want to stick with it, but you know it's time to move on. Maybe that's how Dad felt about living in the city.

DAY TWENTY-ONE

I ran down to the Hazel Wood to see if there was a note, and it was fantastic –

Dear Hazel Wood Girl,

Hmmm. A stick! Ha ha. OK, funny (just about!). Here is a better joke and just as short. What do you call a man with no arms and no legs in a swimming pool? – Bob!'

I know all those ones from my last school. My favourite is – What do you call a woman with one leg? Eileen. Then what do you call a woman with two legs? – Noleen.

 Then the note said,

I am not your dad or Mrs Hooper, or the couple from the Egg Farm (Wow, are they a piece of work or what!?), so keep guessing. Maybe when we meet we can think of something outrageous for you to do.

Another question, Hazel Wood Girl.

What is the best thing that ever happened to you?

From, The Watcher.

I've been thinking about that all day, and I think that the BEST thing that ever happened to me was when I sang a song in front of my family, and all my cousins and uncles and aunts at my Grandad's birthday. I sang one that used to be Grandad's favourite and he hadn't heard it in years and there were tears in his eyes. They all kept telling me how great it was, and telling Mum and Dad that I had a lovely voice and must have got it from their side of the family.

 When I read the note I thought how I haven't really been singing at all lately.

I tried to get into the school choir when we moved here, but you had to audition in front of all the others who were already in the choir, and my voice went all funny and I didn't even finish the song. The teacher was really nice and said to work hard in music class and try again next year, but I heard some of the others laughing so I don't want to be in their stupid choir now. I used to love singing.

DAY TWENTY-TWO

I met the tall guy today (well, sort of), and he looks even better close up. Or maybe he just seems to look better because my brain went all fuzzy with nerves. He was in the supermarket looking at the bread shelves and I was with Mum and not paying attention, so I almost walked into him.

He looked really shocked, I think because I was carrying a sack of sweet potatoes and dropped them when I saw him. He said,

'Hello', and I was so surprised that I just picked up the sweet potatoes, turned around and walked back to Mum. I could hear him laughing at me as I walked away which shows that he's *exactly* like they are in school. Still, I was kicking myself that I didn't say 'Hi' back, or maybe even stand there and say something. I could have suggested a good type of bread or something. No! There, you see, that's as charming and witty as I can imagine myself being, a bread-suggester, and that's so ridiculous! Anyway he probably knows I'm The Farmer and it's everyone's job to not like me.

Then, as if that didn't scramble my head up completely, on the way back to the car I saw Emma-Jo and she was walking hand-in-hand with this guy from the year above me called Beau. They looked so cute together; their hair is almost exactly the same, short and fair and they are the same height. So she isn't going out with the tall guy, or at least I hope not. Not that he would ever like me, but it would be a bit much if she has loads of boyfriends while all the other girls in town are sitting in their greenhouses, dreaming like idiots.

Before the supermarket trip, I left a note down at the Hazel Wood saying about the singing day, the good one at Grandad's party not the whole choir fiasco. I wanted to tell The Watcher about the tall guy laughing at me and how much that hurt, but I can't do that until I know The Watcher's identity. It would be amazing if it was a girl my age (a nice one) and I could tell her about things.

I just this minute went down to the Hazel Wood again, and there was already a note there. It says –

Dear Hazel Wood Girl,

Thank you for telling me about your singing. I'm sure you sounded incredible.

The best thing that ever happened to me was when my dad took me fishing and we sat for hours, sometimes talking and sometimes not. He caught a huge trout and I helped him reel it in, and caught it in the net at the very end. When we got home he told Mum and everyone else that I had caught it, even though it was really him.

Question: If you could meet one person from history who would it be and why?

From, The Watcher.

I wonder if JL counts as a person from history. It feels weird, like I have a friend even though I have never met them. I kidded myself for a while that it might be the tall guy but I know that I never have that kind of luck.

I am an idiot

DAY TWENTY-THREE

I HAVE FINALLY REALISED. I am an idiot, like as if that's news. When I woke up this morning, in one single brain-spasm it became glaringly obvious that Barbara and her friends thought of the whole Hazel Wood Girl thing. It's *so* obvious that they will be showing my notes all around school, and laughing at me again, and putting them on the noticeboards. I know she's away, but I bet she paid someone to do this to me. Why? What did I ever do to any of them?

I wish everyone would either be my friend or leave me alone properly. I feel horrible and wish I could get back to just feeling numb.

*****

I did about an hour of French and then sat there looking at the stupid cows. Sammy-boy was doing the same thing from near their house on the other side of the field (staring, not learning French) and for some reason I got up and wandered over. As usual, he had his hands in front of his mouth with his sleeve-ends pulled up over his fingers, so I could just make it out when he said,

'Mum said to ask would you like to come for tea today?'

I was in the mood for nice normal people so I said,

'Love to.'

And he said,

'Come on then,' through his sleeves.

It was good to sit and talk to Mrs Hooper. It made me feel I could be anywhere. Little Sammy-boy is so adorable. He really loves wild animals, and before I left he told me about a hedgehog he found and has been feeding on worms in their back garden.

Her other young son, Christophe, wasn't there, and I am pretty certain that maybe Mrs Hooper has invented a second kid for the purposes of child-support money or some kind of tax relief.

I die inside whenever I think of the girls from school being behind the notes. Why can't they just like me?

DAY TWENTY-FOUR

I almost *fainted*. It was eight o'clock in the morning and I was in the kitchen in my red long t-shirt that I wear to bed, and my old sweat pants from four years ago that are really too small, and the tall guy walked through our farmyard!!!!!!!!!!!!!!!!!!!!

He talked to Adam for a few minutes and then walked off back down the lane. I couldn't even *move*. I'm just so grateful that (especially with me in my PJs) he didn't come into the house or he would never have spoken to me again. Not that he ever has, or would, but you know what I mean.

There are some guys that speak to you, and some that don't. I bet he's the kind that only talks to whatever girl they want to snog that night, or whoever is the most popular or can do something for them. So that's me out on all counts, but him walking through the farmyard is still the best thing to happen since that day in early spring when Dad finally worked out the heating.

Anyway, I am now dressed (too nicely dressed for an ordinary day – sad and pathetic or what??), and am going to find out what he was doing here. Maybe he is one of the people stealing the veggies and eggs and stuff. Mum thinks the magpies are doing it, but I think that's the defense lawyer in her coming out again.

***

OK. Maybe, just *maybe* my life is not completely cursed! I just now went and asked Adam and Dad what that guy was doing in the yard and Dad said,

'You mean Christophe Hooper?'

And then I got it. The tall guy is Mrs Hooper's other son. I AM IN SHOCK!! Real shock, the kind they give you brandy for when you're older.

But it's all a bit messed up in my head because I thought Christophe was about ten and the tall guy is at least fifteen, so I was really confused. I think that because there's two years between me and Mindy I presumed that Christophe must be two years older than Sammy-boy, or something. Maybe it was because Adam said 'little boys', and suggested I babysit. I suppose he didn't know either at the time.

I have no clue really.

Anyway, once Mindy gets back they will be best friends because they are both about the same age and she's popular, and I'll be left out. I'm not going to even try to be friends with him because I'll just end up being disappointed.

So the tall guy is Christophe Hooper and he is my neighbour. I wonder if maybe he knows Barbara and she got him to collect notes from me so that she could use him to help make a fool of me.

I bet he's The Watcher.

I'm not going to write back.

DAY TWENTY-FIVE

I was up and dressed and staring out the kitchen window by seven and finally gave up at eight-thirty with a big, long day stretching in front of me. So I was lucky that FINALLY I've got something to do. Dad is way more of a softie than Mum, and when I begged him, he let me help get some papers together for a business meeting to do with ownership of the farm.

Adam is not exactly a business genius and I spent the morning scrabbling around for contracts and letters in the dining-room/office, and found most of them inside old farming magazines and between unpaid bills from the last century almost.

It was a bit of a shocker to realise that Dad is now in charge of the whole farm. I presumed Adam would be here forever, and that Dad would get so frustrated with the whole muddy mess of farming that one morning he'd wake us up and tell us to pack to return to the city. But, as well as finding out that the farm is now Dad's, Adam told us at lunch that he's got a job in the Far East teaching English-as-a-foreign-language. He's going at the end of the summer.

This is beyond horrible, my worst nightmare. It feels like a stone sitting in my stomach and like my head is full of nothing but air. Maybe I can run away and become a film star and divorce my parents or whatever they call that. I really hate it here, more than I have ever hated anything, even more than I used to hate violin lessons with the old shouty lady. Farms are fine for little kids, boring people, and old people, but not for teenagers and not for people with dreams and an imagination. I cannot spend a whole summer looking out the kitchen window in case my cute neighbour (who, as if I need reminding, laughed at me like I was the fool of the universe the only time we met) might decide to walk past.

I think Dad could tell I was in a not-good way, and he brought me to the meeting in the town hall with his lawyer and some other people; I don't really know who they were. The lawyer made a joke about us being there to sign me over to a new family and I found the idea appealing.

The town hall was a good place to get away from things because it looks like it's from somewhere far away, even though it's on the main street. It's like a red-brick, German-fairytale castle from a horror movie, super-old and small with turrets, arches, carved wooden banisters and panelling, and mosaic tiles on the floor.

My backside was in bits waiting on the hard mahogany benches in reception because Dad is always on time for things and the rest of the world is always late. The secretary was really lovely to us, and even in the middle of the meeting she came in with more tea, and gave me the last of the chocolate wafer biscuits.

Meetings are where people take two hours to say things that could be said in two minutes. The best I can tell, it was about some legal contract with the Egg Farm Grangers, who own the stone barn at the edge of our farm, the one right across the little road from their house and chicken sheds. They lease out the big, stone barn to us (like renting it to us) and Dad says it's the best one for storing hay.

For all their shiny shoes they didn't know much. The lawyer has no clue if the Grangers even *own* the barn that we are paying them to use. That would be like me collecting rent money for hiring out the café. A bit on the cheeky side to say the least. If that *is* true than the person that *really* owns the stone barn could find out and run us off with hunting rifles. Well, they didn't say that last part, but I bet that could happen. People get funny about their stuff. Like the way Mum is getting pissed off with all the food disappearing from our kitchen garden.

We have started calling it, 'The Murderous Mystery of the Vanishing Vegetables'. Dad thinks that it might be a homeless person passing through, except now it's been happening for more than a week. I think it must be animals. It's not the same as dogs in the city that eat tinned dog food, or stuff from the deli if their owners are rich enough. The animals here are not polite. A whole row of the early spinach went missing this morning and some of the broad beans. Dad says that small clumps of green wheat have been disappearing too.

Anyway, the *actual* real news of the day is that the secretary at the town hall said that she has a daughter my age, and why don't I come for dinner tomorrow night. Dad said, 'Yes', for me, because I didn't know what to say. I must learn to just say something and then sort out how I feel about it later.

I *do* want to go, but I'm scared, in fact terrified, in case her daughter is someone from my school, someone who calls me The Farmer and expects me to scratch my head with my knife and fork. Idiot me didn't think to ask her daughter's name. It might be OK, the mum seems really nice and who knows, I might get a few chocolate-wafer biscuits for my trouble.

It's not much to ask. Just one full day with no surprises. Please.

DAY TWENTY-SIX

The Watcher a note left on the greenhouse door, which *weirded* me *out*. I mean, how did they know that I hang out there?

It started with –

Dear Hazel Wood Girl,

I hope everything is all right. Please leave a note here if for some reason you can't make it to the Hazel Wood.

Then The Watcher answered the question from the last note, which made me feel bad for not replying.

It said –

If I could meet one person from history it would be Elvis, so I could ask him how it felt to be the most popular singer in the world. I love singing too and playing guitar. Since remembering about catching the trout, I have decided to spend today fishing. Please just let me know that you are OK.

From, The Watcher.

Right. Now I think it *must* be Christophe, but what if it isn't? I have no clue what to do. No clue whatsoever. I think I just want it to be him because I know he'd never talk to me.

Sammy-boy was wandering like a lost lamb again so I invited him to join me in the greenhouse and gave him some markers and drawing paper. He drew me this amazing picture of a hedgehog and we stuck it up on the wooden tray. I asked him how old his brother is, and he said,

'Just turned sixteen.'

I'd bet every chocolate biscuit in the known universe that it is Christophe sending the notes, pretending to want to be my friend. I bet he's doing it to get in with Barbara and her lot. But why would he say things about himself if it was all just to get me in trouble with Barbara? I am now even more extra confused, and that's saying something.

I have been writing in this to take my mind off the fact that Adam is driving me to that lady's house in about ten minutes to have dinner with her and her daughter. I really wish I didn't have to go, nothing is ever worth the worry. Adam is seeing 'Liza' again (Miss Dobbs, who I remember had a habit of wagging her foot until it almost came off) and when I asked him about going to the Far East and leaving her here, he just said that the end of the summer is a long time away. That is so like a man! *So* not romantic. They think romance is something you buy, like chocolates and flowers, when your woman gets too whingy.

***

LATER

OK. Good stuff! All marvellous enough for the meantime! Yes, I think I might even have my first ... well not *friend* exactly, but at least someone to hang out with. And it's the famous Emma-Jo of all people. Talk about strange and weird and everything. It turns out she's the town hall secretary's daughter, and I felt this huge mix of thrilled and freaked when I saw her perched up by their kitchen table. But she looked OK with me being there, so I could tell that she didn't know she was supposed to hate me, so at least I have a little bit of time. Fingers crossed she doesn't talk to Barbara on the phone too much.

We disappeared off into the den after eating, while her mum stayed in the kitchen, so we could talk *really,* not just that way you do in front of parents. Emma-Jo is easily the best person I have EVER met. Before now I've never come across anyone who is so, I don't know, so *in charge* of themselves. I know that sounds stupid, but she really knows what she likes and doesn't like and she says it. She's crazy into all these old rock bands from when our parents were young, and new ones that have that same guitar sound. It felt like a few minutes, but really it was two hours that we sat and listened to their stuff, with Emma-Jo almost exploding with excitement telling me the deep meaning behind all the lyrics. It's a bit different to the indie bands we all used to listen to in the city.

Her life's big dream is to be a rock star and to live exactly in the same area where we used to live, and I told her all about the shops and people and how much there was going on there, and she couldn't get enough of it. I think it was the first time that I actually said out loud how much I miss being busy and excited about stuff. She feels the same way as I do about so little going on around here. We agreed that if someone made a film about this place it would have to be one of those very boring arty films with a Norwegian voiceover and dodgy subtitles and lots of gaps and silences with wind blowing and bad clothes.

Just as we could hear my dad driving up outside, she told me a huge secret, that she and her boyfriend Beau are starting up a rock band so they have something fun to do this summer. Emma-Jo already looks like a rock star, even the way she sits and talks and everything. When I think back right now about how much I was talking tonight, I'm a bit worried that maybe I sounded boring or silly. But then, maybe what I said was OK because she kept listening and she's not the sort to let herself be bored.

She asked me did I play any instrument, but I don't (thanks to the violin devil lady).

I *so* wanted to offer to help out, to maybe make posters or help them think of a name for the band, but I didn't think she would want me involved so I said nothing (big surprise there then!). I also didn't ask her about knowing Christophe because I wouldn't know what to say if she asked me if I know him.

I am trying not to think of him at all. But not doing all that well, it would seem.

DAY TWENTY-SEVEN

When we woke up this morning there was a bunch of HUGE fish on our doorstep! Luckily they were in a basket with a lid, so Trug didn't get to them. I knew in a second that The Watcher was at work. Mum is a bit freaked out because so many of the strawberries have gone missing and now these big, fat fish have landed on her. Well, not *on* her, but she feels she has to fillet them and cook them for dinner so they don't go to waste. Dad says we'll have a barbecue tonight and make the fish the main course. I used to love when we'd have them back home, and everyone we knew would come over and we'd take over the lounge with all our friends while the adults were on the balcony.

Emma-Jo just phoned, and asked me to help her set-up the auditions to find a lead guitarist and a singer for her band! She said she reckons I'm really good at thinking things through, which *I* reckon is another way of calling me shy and mousy. Emma-Jo plays bass guitar (which is so cool, I would give anything to be that cool, although I don't want to play guitar because I tried it once and it killed my fingers), and Beau plays drums. Or as Emma-Jo says,

'Well, he hits them, bless him.'

I said that I'd ask my dad if we can hold the auditions in one of the barns. I'll ask him tomorrow after he's had breakfast and done that thing where he pats his stomach with both hands and goes, 'Ah yes, this is the good life!' Sometimes when my dad is being a complete embarrassment like that, Mum sees me making a face and whispers, 'At least he's not dancing!', which always makes me smile again. He dances like he's pulled several important muscles and flaps his arms around with his mouth hanging open. We have geese that dance better than Dad.

I'm *ridiculously* excited now that I have a task, and

finally know some people. I hope Christophe won't tell Emma-Jo that I'm a loser who drops bags of sweet potatoes and wanders about in the wood, because that would ruin everything. I have decided that he *must* be The Watcher, must be.

I still haven't answered the last note.

They gave me the job of asking the Hoopers over for the fish barbecue at our place tonight and I am *dying* at the thought of it. I asked Adam would he do it and he said he had to get the fence-mending finished and then go and collect Liza. So basically, I have to eat fish and listen to my mother getting tipsy on red wine, while the most fanciable guy in the world, and a teacher from my school watch me.

Okaaaaay, brilliant.

DAY TWENTY-EIGHT

Not only did I survive last night, but it was even a bit good. We sat outside the kitchen door in the little bit of yard in front of the kitchen garden, which Mum calls the patio, but is really just a hard bit of ground with no grass. Sammy-boy had his hedgehog with him to show us. Now that I have met Emma-Jo I feel bad for Sammy-boy having no one his age to play with.

Mum was not too loud and only drank a bit of wine, not like at the parties in the city. Liza (who I accidentally called Miss Dobbs three times) is hilarious and had us all in stitches with her stories about different schools she has taught in. She did a perfect impression of the headmaster at my school and I thought I would fracture my insides from laughing so much. I actually talk when she is around because she asks me loads of questions about myself. I like that. So, Liza's on my party-list, for certain, even though she's an adult. It's going to be weird if she's my teacher again.

I managed not to have to talk to Christophe all night and he looked *way* more embarrassed than me any time we caught each other's eye. I guess it was a real come-down for him to have to hang out with not cool people like me and my family, but why did he leave the fish and the notes if he doesn't want to have anything to do with me? If he *is* the Watcher, of course; I don't know whether I'd be disappointed or relieved if he wasn't! He must be though! Must. He mostly spoke to Dad and they seemed to be having fun. He talks fast, laughs a lot and waves his arms about like an Italian when he's explaining things. He is SO gorgeous (she mentioned for the fifty thousanth time!), I'm glad I didn't have to sit beside him or I'd have been too nervous to eat.

Then, I was bringing some of the dirty plates back into the kitchen, and he followed me because his mum made him collect some too. So we were both there in the kitchen and had put the plates down. He had no interest whatsoever in talking to me and just as he was headed out to the 'patio' again I panicked and blurted,

'Thanks for the fish!'

Of course he just laughed at me again and didn't look back.

He didn't deny that it was him, but made it very clear that it wasn't something he wanted to be made known to people. So I'm good enough to be a note-leaving friend, but not good enough to be a real social friend? I guess he's as bored as I am and it's a way of doing something without having to actually hang out with me. Kind of like the way Barbara spoke to me on the way to school then dropped me like a too-hot cheese-toastie as soon as others were around.

Then Liza, Adam and Mum came into the kitchen so I couldn't dwell on the fiasco of my first attempt at a conversation with Christophe. Mum organised us all into getting the fruit flan together for dessert. My mum should be in charge of China, or a medium-sized country at the very least. Her talent is seriously wasted on such a small party, on such a small farm, on a fruit flan. Seriously.

When they were leaving the Hoopers hugged us all because they are a huggy family even though we aren't. Because everyone ended up hugging everyone goodbye I know that the (really fast and not very huggy) hug Christophe gave me didn't mean anything except a goodbye hug. So I'm not blowing it out of proportion or anything. It was nice to get any kind of hug though, for a minute it looked like he was just going to leave me out.

Anyway ... today Sammy-boy hung out with me in the greenhouse all afternoon. It's finally comfortable and not just bearable since I moved down the old chairs from my bedroom, and found a broken side-table top that Sammy can rest over the arms of his chair for drawing on. I made us a picnic lunch of tuna and sweetcorn sandwiches and Sammy drew a picture of us all at the barbecue, which is great (except I look a bit like a hamster for some reason). I insisted he sign that and the hedgehog one, which seemed to make him really happy, so I got him to write a sign saying 'The Gallery', which we put on the greenhouse door. At least *he's* happy to hang out with me!

Tonight I just lay on my bed, did a few minutes of French and then just sort of lay there again.

OK, not to bang on about the hug thing, but I think

it proves (as if proof were needed) that Christophe couldn't ever fancy me, because when you fancy someone you get way too self-conscious about hugging them. Not that I mind or anything. Just saying.

God, shut-up Poppy, he thinks you are a social rash! Stop wanting people to like you when it's obvious they think you're a waste of space!

I just can't stop thinking about him and have re-read the Watcher notes over and over.

DAY TWENTY-NINE

Emma-Jo likes hanging out with me, that's one thing at least. Emma-Jo is the kind of person you could put in a bottle and sell as an energy drink. Good thing I didn't leave this out by the bed because I was woken up at seven-thirty this morning by her landing into my bedroom like a tornado.

'Morning, chick! Let's get famous!'

'What time is it?'

'Time to *seriously* rumble with the audition thing!'

I dragged on some jeans and a t-shirt and ran downstairs to fetch us a breakfast of banana-nut muffins and a huge pot of orange-pekoe tea to have in my bedroom on the sheepskin rugs.

That's a wonderful thing about living in this farmhouse, my bedroom is HUGE. It used to be the attic, and although the ceiling is low, it's about three times bigger than the other bedrooms. Mindy and I chose who would sleep where, without ever having been here, just hearing descriptions. So Mindy got the room with the farmyard view, which isn't as good as it sounds from far away in the city. When we got here and she realised that hers was tiny and really noisy in the mornings, she tried to force me to swap. But Dad took charge, and said that she had fought for her room when she thought it was the best, and that I had every right to stay where I was.

So anyway, — *get to the point, Poppy*!

Emma-Jo cleared her throat and announced,

'Poppy, chick, there has been a meeting. A businesslike, professional, business meeting with pens and everything, and the result is that Beau and I have decided *you* should be our Marketing girl for the first gig. We're talking posters, parades, coupons, whatever it takes to get those bums in the doors and on the seats.'

'Yes, great! Love to,' was all I could manage without choking on a muffin.

We went on to have the *best* time planning how to hold the auditions for her band. I'm going to show people in, and get their names and phone numbers, and take a photo of them so we can remember who is who. Then Emma-Jo and Beau will sit behind a table, listen to each person play, and ask them about their influences and if they have time to rehearse, and suss out if they are serious about it.

I can't believe this is happening so fast. Part of me is scared that when Beau sees me he'll know who I am and tell Emma-Jo that they laugh at me and call me The Farmer at school. But at least I am still involved for now.

This afternoon I went down to the Hazel Wood and there was a note from The Watcher pinned to the tree. Well, from Christophe, but I still think of him as The Watcher when I'm in the wood. I was worried that he was going to stop now that I am 90 per cent certain of his identity.

It said:

Dear Hazel Wood Girl...

And instead of a note there was this amazing

black-and-white hand-drawn cartoon of me wearing the outfit I had on last night. He had exaggerated my eyes and made them look incredible. He had my hair even more wild, long and curly than it is in real life, and I was standing in a field of cows, getting butted by one. It also had no mouth, which I suppose is a dig at me not talking much. And he didn't make me look like a hamster. It was so fantastic that I wanted to show it to someone, but then I would have had to explain about me being the Hazel Wood Girl and Christophe being The Watcher, so I just ran up to my bedroom and taped it to the side of the old mahogany wardrobe, where I can see it from my bed, but no one else can see it if they walk into my room.

I know I should be angry with him for not wanting to talk to me or be my friend in the real world, but compared to not having him be my friend at all, this is good enough. If I was less of an idiot, dropping things and saying 'Thanks for the fish', instead of 'Hi, I'm Poppy', then maybe he might be bothered with me one day rather than have me as a part-time project just because they don't have a TV. I still think that maybe it's some trick, but right now I'm going to try to just enjoy it.

New plan – I am definitely going to talk more. This is the ideal time because Mindy is away and not taking up all the airspace. I just have to get over this notion that everyone has good things to say and I don't. When you think about it, most things most people say are just ordinary, and that's OK. Most of my old friends knew me from when I was a baby, but to make new ones you have to ask questions and tell people about who you are inside.

DAY THIRTY

Today I said more than I normally would in a whole month. Most of this talking happened in the café in town, which is unofficially our rock band office, as long as we buy a fresh pot of tea every hour. Quite a good rate for office space these days! Beau is much less scary than I thought he'd be. When he talks, he says things in this long drawn-out way which makes him sound like he just woke up all the time. The fact that neither of them had any idea that I'm usually practically mute, meant that they didn't think it was weird of me to say so much. That felt good. It's like I can be my real self with them, not the person I accidentally ended up being.

Emma-Jo has decided that her name is not rock

star enough, and we all have to call her 'Em-J', which does have a good sound to it. Beau knows that his name means 'handsome' in French, and so he loves it. I think I already have a cool name, it's just that I need to grow into it.

Once we were all clear on what to call each other, I said,

'My dad's OK with us using the big, stone barn.'

'Why do you have a special barn for the big stones?' asked Beau, and he wasn't joking either.

'It's a big barn, made of stone rather than bricks or wood,' Em-J explained patiently, 'hence "big, stone barn".'

And you got the feeling that she spent a lot of time filling him in on the basics. It's obvious she adores him though. It's like they balance each other out, she brings him up to her high speed, and then he calms her down with a big smile and a kiss.

Em-J wrote out the audition notice, which says:

Lead guitarist and singer needed for new, impossibly awesome rock band. Only people with the spirit, skills and super-style of a rock god or goddess may apply. Dare to display your super star-self if you drip with attitude and reek of success.

And then we added where and when, and that there would be no food. Adam says people always expect to get fed, so I thought we better put that in case they went wandering over to the house for refreshments. I can just imagine Mum wrestling with complete strangers for control of the coffee pot. Not a good picture.

While me and Em-J shared a slice of pecan pie and talked about the artistic direction of the band (and about boys and hair lighteners), Beau went off to get a dozen copies of the audition notice printed up. Em-J voted amongst herself and decided that I should be the band's official production manager. Not objecting too furiously is the same thing as agreeing as far as Em-J is concerned, so I suppose I agreed.

By the time Beau came back Em-J had pretty much planned the first world tour and written it up on a napkin, between the pastry crumbs. I just love the way she calls everyone 'chick', even Beau.

We had the most hilarious time going around convincing people to put our audition notices in the newsagent's window, the noticeboard in the supermarket, beside the maps and things in the reception area of the town hall, even sticking the last few up on trees and lampposts along the main street.

I did the asking in most places because I am the production manager, and because the other two think I look like the least trouble. I know that means that they don't think I'm nearly as edgy as them, and they'd be right.

It was so funny, they would start slyly poking me in the back or tugging on my hair as I was talking, to try and make me laugh or mess up what I was saying. I can't stop laughing now, just thinking about it.

Em-J is *so* into things being stunning and all outer-atmosphere, that I'm certain she must find me really dull. Anyway, I suppose she needs me for now and that's good enough. BIG plus, is that Beau is too dozy to have noticed that they don't like me in school, so – as long as Barbara Montague stays away and doesn't phone – I'm safe as houses for the summer. Unless the new people in the band know about me ... God! How did I manage to be one of the hated ones? I was always one of the liked ones before, always, even if I wasn't the princess of the planet or anything.

DAY THIRTY-ONE

I was down at the Hazel Wood early this morning, just as the sun came up over the ruined cottage, not looking for a note, just enjoying looking at the trees like when I first went down there. I wandered around and thought of how much things are different just because of knowing Em-J. It so rocks, how she has an idea and makes it happen. Also the way she makes everything sound so huge, 'We're talking global domination, chick,' 'Millions of raving fans, BRING IT *ON!*' I've never had a friend before that makes me feel so much like doing things. So in that mood I decided to get tough with The Watcher (now 99 per cent sure it's Christophe). Dangerously, I had brought pen and paper with me, so I wrote;

Dear Watcher,

So, if this 'thing' with us is going to only exist in the Hazel Wood, you won't mind sending me flowers instead of just notes. Right?

Yours,

HWG

I think I was annoyed with him and feeling confident at the same time and wanting him to think I was really 'couldn't care less' about it all. I loved myself for it for the first half hour because it seemed like such an Em-J, kick-ass thing to do, but then I was worried sick all day that he'd think the note was lame. I might have ruined everything and even though he doesn't want to know me, I now look forward to the notes instead of daydreaming about JL. I was too worried to even go and get it back in case he was already reading it while I came along. Flowers? God! What possessed me to ask for flowers!? At the time, things can seem like *such* a good idea, but the better you think the idea is at first, the more you worry that it's crap once the excitement has worn off.

Mum asked me to keep a lookout over the kitchen garden today as so much stuff is disappearing, which gave me more time for brooding.

Sammy-boy sat with me and the pair of us were in it together because he looked really sad and worried too, but we both cheered up a bit after I fetched us slices of lemon poppy-seed cake almost the size of our own heads. It turned out he didn't know that a poppy is a flower, so seeing as Mum was back by then and no foreign armies had invaded the kitchen garden, I said let's go to the big, stone barn where some poppies grow wild. When we got there he sat sketching the poppies (which looked amazing because there were about two dozen of them against the long grass at the back of the stone barn) and I walked around the building.

My plan was to check that it's in a fit state for the audition. It's just right where our farm finishes, across a small road from the Egg Farm, about half a mile from the Hazel Wood and a quarter of a mile from our main house. It's the darkest building in the district and I hated coming here last winter. Dad says the Grangers are really angry because our lawyers are questioning paying for the use of the barn, so to keep away from them. Like as if I was about to invite myself over for tea!

OK, I know it's just my imagination making a drama out of nothing (and then pouring some more mystery sauce on top of that), *but* I was a bit freaked when I saw loads of footprints in the compacted earth below the single barn window. That was weird because there were no footprints around the big double door, and the window is up so high that you could never get in there from the ground. Inside it was all just left-over bales of hay from last winter and a couple of plastic pails. I noticed that the bales were all turned over, as if someone had been looking underneath them. Or maybe just bales get turned over.

Anyway, back to reality. I suppose Em-J and Beau can just sit on the bales as they audition people.

On the way back Sammy-boy told me that Christophe works for a farmer across town at different times of the day depending on what needs doing, which explains why I don't see him all that much. Mum told me that the Hoopers used to live on a noisy housing estate where Mrs Hooper was worried that the boys would start hanging out with a bad crowd.

I wonder if his work will mean he can't audition for

Em-J's band (but if he got into the band then Em-J and Beau would ignore me to talk to him, and he'd probably convince them to get someone better to do the organising).

There I go! Inventing problems ahead of time.

I must ask Em-J what the name of the band will be. Bands are only ever as good as their names, so if a band is called something crap you can pretty much know they'll be torture to listen to. I think the simple names are the best.

Tomorrow is audition day! I am *so* nervous I don't think I'll be able to sleep.

DAY THIRTY-TWO

We got to the barn a while before we were due to start and already there were at least twenty people of all ages, shapes and sizes. Half with guitars, shuffling around in their best boots, and millions of earrings, and all looking like this was their one big chance to make something of themselves. There was lots of nail-biting, gum-chewing and hair-twisting going on. Mum didn't let us borrow the dining room chairs when I asked, which was fair enough considering all the muck around the place. I mean the actual mud outside the barn, the people were lovely! And no one seemed to mind standing or sitting on the ground, looking out across the Egg Farm one way and our farm yard the other way. (We were lucky there was no Granger activity all day.) It looked a bit odd really, rocker-invasion down at the farm, the same way a pig walking down the main street of a city would look kind of out of place.

The first half of the morning had me crazy-busy taking names and getting photos done, so I didn't pay much attention to how people were performing.

From the start we called them 'the hopefuls' rather than 'the auditionees', but after a while Em-J started to call them 'the hopeless', which gave me a clue as to how things were going! 'The hopeless' all seemed to be much younger or much older than us, and I didn't recognise anyone from school. I even noticed one of the waitresses from the café there, wearing jeans that were *way* too tight for her, and it didn't seem to help her singing either. There was one *really* gorgeous guy called Glynn, who was *so* incredibly stylish that when he walked in I could tell Beau was torn between being happy for the band and worried that Em-J might fancy him. But he couldn't sing to save his life, so that sorted that. I wondered if it was OK to keep the photos and numbers for personal use. Probably not. Mum would call it unethical. But then Dad would call it entrepreneurial.

Remembering what a tough time I had at the try-outs for the school choir, I made the extra effort to tell everyone 'great job', and to say 'thank you so much', when they were leaving. I was really confident and chatty. Well done, me! I think I will go to the kitchen right now and reward myself with a soy yoghurt.

***

Yoghurt devoured.

***

Oh my God, this one girl brought her piano-accordion and it was all I could do not to laugh at Em-J and Beau's 'serious faces' while she played, 'Danny Boy', all the way through. When they asked her if she knew any rock songs she said she didn't like rock music, which is a little unexpected at a rock band audition.

About four cute-ish guys showed up, but they had obviously only started to learn guitar as soon as they saw the audition notice, and were looking at their hands the whole time, and taking forever to change from one chord to another.

There were loads of groups of nine-year-old girls

who giggled more than they sang.

My personal favourite was the ten-year-old boy and girl twins playing recorders; their mother brought them and stood beside them holding her baby, while they struggled through a verse and a chorus of 'Greensleeves'. When Beau and Em-J didn't invite her precious darlings straight into the band, the mother started shouting at them and saying she'd report them to the police for wasting people's time.

When the last person left and I closed the door and gave the thumbs-up, we all just burst out laughing and were rolling around in hysterics in the hay.

'OK,' Em-J finally said. 'There must be *one* kick-ass person our age in this town who can sing.'

'What about Poppy?' asked Beau.

In order to get that thought *right* out of their heads I blurted,

'Christophe Hooper, he plays guitar and loves singing, he's a big Elvis fan.'

Em-J clapped her hands together,

'Perfect!' she said, and she marched out of the big, stone barn followed by a confused Beau and a relieved me.

She quizzed me as we traipsed across to the Hooper's place.

'How do you know?'

'How do I know what?'

'A) Christophe Hooper and B) that he can sing and play guitar and C) that he likes Elvis. Poppy, chick, that's a lot of knowing for someone whose said nothing about him the whole time we've been planning.'

'Friend of the family ... I, um, just found out,' I muttered, and she let it go.

I really hope he is The Watcher and that he isn't all, 'What? I don't play guitar!' When I think about it, he hasn't actually officially admitted to it being him. He wasn't in (thank God) so we left him a note with Mrs Hooper and a voice mail message too.

OK, I'm now exhausted after writing all that. Off to sleep. And after today I'll probably dream out of tune.

DAY THIRTY-THREE

In spite of all the stern talkings-to that I have given myself, I still completely fancy Christophe, and he is not helping matters by probably being The Watcher. As soon as I think of how he is when we're in the same space, I hate him, and then he goes and does something cool as The Watcher and I fall for him all over again. I know he would never go for someone like me, but it's nice to have him around to practise fancying someone local. Does that make sense?

Anyway, this morning I brought a muffin and an apple down to the Hazel Wood for breakfast, and there was a huge piece of paper hanging from the usual note-tree. I could see it from ages away, and ran the last bit. The piece of paper was easily half the size of me, and on it was drawn a huge bunch of flowers, really detailed, coloured every colour of the rainbow and signed 'The Watcher'. It's my first ever bunch of flowers (except for when I was Mum's friend's flower girl when I was three!), and I don't care that it's a drawing. Or that it's a neighbourly gift and not a romantic one. I don't care, I *love* it!

Again, it sort of proves he thinks of me as a (sort of) friend, because otherwise he wouldn't have been able to just do it, but hey, I'm not exactly sad at having a new (sort of) friend, after all the fun and games at school. I hope it makes Mindy jealous when she gets to be his girlfriend.

I sat there looking at it as I ate my breakfast, and then ran back to the house and upstairs to store it in my room. Then Dad drove me over to Em-J's house for the next band meeting, and I waltzed in and was *mortified,* because Christophe was sitting there talking about music with Beau. While I recovered by helping Em-J squeeze some oranges for juice, she explained that Christophe was really into being in the band, and could rehearse in the mornings and late evenings. She said it was a pity I didn't play an instrument, and I told her that I'm much happier helping out in other ways.

I stayed and listened while they rehearsed a song that Em-J wrote called 'Climbing Tall Ladders', and Christophe made it sound wonderful by inverting the chords. Em-J even took up my idea for changing a couple of the lyrics, which made me feel involved. Of course Christophe didn't even look at me once or speak to me or anything, so it proves what I thought about me not being cool enough for him.

The only part of the rehearsal that *didn't* work was deciding on a band name. 'Blue Thunder', 'The Rock Stars', and something like 'Crawfish Maniacs', were some of the ideas, but we never got closer than each person liking the name that they thought of, and not liking the other ideas. I didn't dare come up with an idea because I didn't want to give Christophe the chance to laugh at it.

At one point Em-J was working out a backing vocal and said,

'Poppy it's a shame you don't sing a bit.'

I said nothing, just smiled fakely, while Christophe stared at me long and hard. I didn't look over and he didn't give me away, which I'm really glad about. At least I now know 100 per cent for absolute certain that he is The Watcher. I think I like that. I think I *really* like that.

He is SO funny the way he teases Em-J for being so rocker, and Beau for being so laid back. I wish I had something good about me that would make me worth teasing too. If I was to tease him it would be about the way he jokes around so much with the others. I think it would take some kind of war to wipe the everlasting smile off his face.

Christophe headed off on his bike at noon, and I finally felt like I could breathe again. I stayed on for a couple of hours with Em-J and Beau and we listened to music and read magazines and just chilled.

Then Adam came to collect me. That's the really rough thing about living in the sticks, you need adults to get you places.

When I got back, Mum was in the living room flicking through seed catalogues and I was so excited telling her how kick-ass the rehearsal was that I didn't care that she wasn't really listening.

I was *so* grateful and happy that I got to hang out with Beau and Em-J and so sad that Christophe always ignores me, that later in the afternoon I sat on my bed and couldn't stop crying. Good tears and then sad tears and then back again. I cried and cried until my throat was ragged. As soon as I'd pull myself together again, anything I looked at or thought about would just set me off again.

It was like all those times when people were mean to me had got stored up inside, and then I just let it all out in one go. Now and then I was also smiling and laughing at the same time, so it would have looked a bit psycho if anyone had seen me. In the end I stopped fighting it and got under the covers and cried it all out until I fell asleep for a while.

I have decided that I will never let people make me feel left out again. I am not going to take any more notes from The Watcher. I am going to show him that I won't be treated like dirt any more.

Later, I went down to the greenhouse. Sammy-boy wasn't around, but I noticed he had brought over some fantastic history books and Neville Shute novels, with a piece of copy-book paper saying,

'From my Mum for keepsies.'

in his almost joined-up writing, which is *so* sweet.

Liza joined us for tea and I really like her. She is so free with how she jokes around and talks and gets excited. She was asking me questions about things and we were talking so much that Adam said,

'Hey, do I get to talk to my girlfriend too?'

Which is great because that means she is officially his girlfriend so I'll get to see her again.

I know this will sound pathetic, but after she left I went up to my room and stood in front of the full-length mirror and practised looking confident and talking in a smiley way. I went from being Liza to being Em-J and then to being me, but with loads of attitude. I finally get that there's no point having cool stuff going on in your head if you don't share it with the world. People only push you around if you let them. I'll show Christophe Hooper that I don't need him or his notes! I used to think it was OK that what happens in the Hazel Wood doesn't really exist outside, but now I know I deserve better. Last Christmas I saw a movie called *Sabrina* where the girl was nothing much and then she went off to live in Paris and when she came back a few years later, she was elegant and stunning, and the men were making fools of themselves over her. Maybe that's what needs to happen to me.

Now that my hair is really long the curls are not so tight and it actually looks good. The sun has made it a bit lighter, even without the help of lemons.

DAY THIRTY-FOUR

I went down early again to the Hazel Wood and there was a Watcher note there. It said only one word on the whole page.

It said,

'Sing.'

Well, he doesn't get to tell me what to do!

I even stayed away from the rehearsal at Em-J's, just to show him! Instead I'm with Sammy-boy in the greenhouse and we're reading books and eating raisins and almonds. Mum has forgotten about guarding the kitchen garden, which is a relief because the greenhouse is much more comfy, especially with Hooper cushions added.

LATER

So I was just there in the greenhouse writing in this, when suddenly Dad rushed over all frantic looking. When he saw us sitting there he said, 'Thank God!' and ran back out and over to the house. Then he came back again a minute later and asked Sammy-boy to run over to his house and tell his mother that he's OK. We were a bit confused until he said:

There's been a big fire in the town hall and no one knows if there was anyone trapped inside. Your brother is at Emma-Jo's house, Sammy-boy, they just called with the news about the fire and were worried about Poppy.'

Sammy-boy ran off through the cows.

I was feeling all shaky and said,

'Em-J's mum, she works there!'

Dad then told me that luckily everyone who works there was at a board meeting with people from the tourist office in the hotel across the street. That meant that the only person inside – that they know about – was a college student working as a security guard for the summer. When the fire alarm sounded, this guy rushed out and then ran straight back in to check no one was trapped inside, and ended up in the hospital after breathing in so much smoke. They won't know for a while if any members of the public had wandered in and got trapped. I hope not.

Mum, Dad and Adam went back into town without me. It feels weird, not knowing what's going on.

LATER

Mrs Hooper just dropped by.

She said that Christophe phoned and asked her to make sure I was feeling OK, what with the fire and everything. Just as my heart leaped and I started to feel all good about that, she said,

'I think he and Sammy-boy think of you as their new sister.'

Which thrilled her, but didn't make me feel good. In fact it destroys any hope I might have had that he might one day like me enough to talk to me. But now I know for a fact that he doesn't even see me as friend potential, let alone girlfriend potential, just as an inconvenient little sister. More proof that he and Mindy will be perfect together.

When Mum, Dad and Adam got back we found out

that the inside of the town hall is completely gutted and most of the brickwork on the outside is burnt too, but only the student security guard guy was inside.

Dad said all the locals are really angry and sad, mostly because the old archives were kept there, all the papers that said about who got married, and who died, and who owned what, and who owed what money to who in the olden days, and all the history of the town, old photos, and all that stuff.

I would have thought they would have put it all on computer years ago, but except for the birth, marriage and death stuff, they didn't get around to many of the papers and photos from before the 1970s.

Mrs Hooper went home and we all just sat around really quiet all evening, except for Mum who was on the phone being lawyer-y, helping local people to understand that even if the papers were missing, they were still married and born and all that.

DAY THIRTY-FIVE

Dad drove me into town after breakfast (back to toast now that Mum is too frantic to make muffins), and Em-J and Beau were standing outside the burnt town hall, behind the yellow, plastic tape that the police had put up to keep people back. There were about twenty people there, all staring, one or two crying, and more than that saying stupid things like, 'It's the way they let young people do what they like,' and 'If the voluntary fire brigade was paid, they would have saved it.'

We plonked ourselves down in the café and Em-J

explained that Beau's cousin, Barry Finch, was the student who got hurt. If he gets out of intensive care soon then there's hope.

Beau is massively proud of his cousin for running back inside a burning building to make sure no one was trapped inside, but he's really worried too. You can tell by the way he is sitting up so straight when he's usually slumped over. Beau says that Barry doesn't have any burns, but that he breathed in so much smoke that he was unconscious by the time the fire brigade found him.

Now I understand why Mum and Dad don't want me and Mindy to do things around the farm, they don't want to have us in hospital or worse.

I feel like I want to help make things better again, but don't know what to do.

Em-J says that they haven't the heart to do the band any more and I sort of know how she feels. I'm a bit relieved too that I don't have to put the effort into avoiding Christophe.

Beau went off to be with his aunty and uncle and I hung around town with Em-J for the morning until Dad was going back home. From the café window we watched the police stop random people along the main street, asking questions and taking notes.

Dad was a bit stressy and kept banging the palm of

his hand on the steering wheel, and told me that some of the documents needed to sort out the problem with the big, stone barn were probably in the town hall, so things are even messier on that front. After this month they're going to stop using that barn altogether.

With the fire, and the barn problems, Christophe being weird with me, and the stuff going missing from our farm, everything feels a bit headachy at the moment. Just when things were getting good.

DAY THIRTY-SIX

The police were around at the farm this morning and were asking Mum, Dad and Adam questions for ages. That made me feel scared, like it was closer to us and we might be in trouble, but Mum was all no-nonsense about it, and said that they have to talk to everyone in the town and the outlying farms because that was their job. They had to interview Dad first because he had been spending a lot of time at the town hall.

Luckily we all had alibis (not that we really needed them!). Sammy-boy and I feel like even closer pals because we are each other's alibi. He even drew a picture of the two of us sitting in the greenhouse and a speech bubble coming out of both of our mouths saying, 'We didn't do nothing!' It's so cute I can't help laughing every time I think about it.

Em-J just phoned. She let Christophe know about not doing the band anymore. Barry Finch is going to recover but he'll be in hospital for a few weeks. That means that he won't be able to earn enough money this summer to do his next year of university. It seems so unfair. It's funny how you can care so much about someone you've never met. I wish there was something I could do.

LATER

It's the middle of the night and I just woke up with a GENIUS (if-I-do-say-so-myself) PLAN. If Em-J reforms her band, they can play a concert in the stone barn and use the money collected at the door for Barry! We could make enough that he'll be able to go back to university in September like he originally planned. I just *know* they'll go for it.

It's going to take some major hot milk to get me back to sleep now, I'm buzzing enough to run all the way to Em-J's. Instead I'll phone her first thing. Also, I want to show Christophe that I don't care about him and that he isn't better than me. Maybe if he hangs out with me more he'll want to actually talk to me and then I can just tell him I'm too busy to be his friend. God, my head is like strange soup, all these unidentifiable bits of weirdness floating around endlessly.

DAY THIRTY-SEVEN

I didn't fall asleep for two hours. Every time I tried to think of boring things like rainy car journeys, and cows and sheep, images of a couple of hundred people at a gig in the stone barn would crash about my brain again. Finally, after dawn, I nodded off and ended up sleeping in until ten in the morning, which around here is pretty much the same as sleeping all day.

Em-J wasn't in when I phoned, and Dad wanted me to go with him to visit some farm where they were doing something environmental. So I left messages for her to meet me at the Hazel Wood at nine o'clock tonight, and explained to her how to get there.

I feel like the Hazel Wood is such a magical place that if we do the planning there, then it just *has* to happen. I also want to make it a place where I think about lots of things, not just The Watcher.

It's now six o'clock and I've just had a long bath after the day visiting the green farm.

LATER

I thought I saw Em-J in the middle of the Hazel Wood and went running over, only realising as I got right up close, that it was Christophe. It was a MAJOR cringy moment. We both just mumbled 'Hi', and he said something about Em-J asking him to be there and her being on her way. He was wearing dark, slightly baggy jeans, a long, ripped sweater, and an old pair of sneakers covered in artwork he'd designed himself. It's like ancient symbols done in a cartoon way. He is too cool. I so wanted him to draw on my sneakers like that, but was too shy to ask. In fact, we didn't say anything for the next two minutes. He's so much easier to talk to when he's The Watcher than when he is Christophe and in front of me.

Eventually he decided to speak to me and said, 'Thanks for looking after my brother, he really loves hanging out with you, especially drawing and eating, those are his favourite things to do.'

It didn't occur to me that he'd know what Sammy-boy and I got up to, so that twisted my brain a bit. I just said,

'Oh, yeah.'

Just when I thought that things couldn't get any more awkward, Em-J and Beau rolled up laughing at how lost they had got on the way.

I relaxed a bit once they were there, and so did he, both of us chatting away to them separately. The sun was setting, and the Hazel Wood looked like it was on another world, with a purple, green and orange sky. The birds sounded so loud without people or traffic sounds in the way. Beau suggested we go to the ruined cottage, but I explained that it's dangerous and doesn't have a roof.

Instead we sat on this small space of tufty grass between four of the trees near the centre of the wood. I'd say we looked like a band of Native American's in pow-wow, except Em-J handed around gum, rather than a pipe.

Everyone completely *loved* the idea of having a benefit concert, and they were all relieved to get the band going again. We tried to come up with another venue closer to town, but only the café was a possibility, and that's too small for us to be able to make the kind of money we need. So I'll be asking Mum and Dad about the stone barn.

Christophe even started to glance at me every now and them and almost said something to me before looking over at Em-J at the last second before he said it.

He said,

'OK, we need a name for the band, and if we don't find one tonight we *have* to call ourselves The Twinkle Fairies. That should get us focused.'

'Twinkle Fairies, Christ!' said Beau, and you could hear his head starting to work.

We each wrote a few suggestions, one on top of each of these sheets of paper that I'd brought to take notes. Then we each put a tick at the bottom of the page if we really liked the suggestion (we could tick as many or as few as we wanted), left it if we were just OK with it, and put a cross if we didn't like it. Then we rolled up the end with our mark, so no one could see how the others had rated it. That way no one knew who suggested which one, or who voted what way, and it was all fair.

In the end, Christophe sorted through them and announced that only one suggestion had unanimous ticks. He climbed into one of the hazel trees to make the announcement more official. With a hands-on-knees drum roll from Beau, and the cheers of a roaring crowd from me and Em-J, he said,

'And the name of the greatest rock band in the world is – Farmer!'

We cheered some more, and we all did this crazy dance around the wood making drum and bass sounds. I even eventually owned up to it being me that thought of it, and I love that I have named a real rock band. Now I'll actually feel *good* if they call me The Farmer in school.

It was really late by then, so even though we all wanted to stay, Christophe went back to his place while Beau and Em-J had decaf coffee over at ours and waited for a lift from her dad. I feel that at least now it's not as impossible with me and Christophe as before, that we can at least do this band thing with the others there to talk through. He's OK, just a bit up himself.

Back in our kitchen Em-J said,

'You have such cool ideas, super-chick! I'm so glad you moved here.'

Beau said,

'Yeah!' and looked exhausted from that much.

We talked with Mum, Dad and Adam, and they

have agreed that we can use the big, stone barn for the concert and they are going to help out on the night. Adam is going to feed extra power lines in tomorrow so Farmer can rehearse there. (God, that sounds *so* good!)

Mum said how pleased she is that I have made such lovely friends. Dad is recovering from being called 'chick'.

DAY THIRTY-EIGHT

From the minute the sun first hit the window right up until evening rehearsal, I was working out plans to get a big enough audience to make the gig a success. I came up with every idea short of stopping each person on the main street and begging them on my knees (although I am even keeping that one in reserve). Several ideas got binned early on, including ones that involved Rollerblades, swimsuits and dressing up in a rooster costume. Going down more sophisticated routes, I now have the phone numbers for the local paper, the radio station, the big businesses like the hotel, and all the places where we put the audition notices (except the town hall, of course).

Luckily Mum knows just about everything there is to know on the planet and taught me how to write a press release to send in to the newspapers and media people like the radio station.

'A press release has to be very short because they don't have much time to read things,' Mum explained. 'Be sure to include all the details such as the name of the band, where and when it is, and how much the tickets are. It also has to have something in it that will make it an interesting news story, not just another band putting on a show.'

Mum, Adam and Dad all talked it through in detail with me at lunch time and we decided that what will interest the media is the fact that Beau is in the band and it's to get money for his cousin, and the fact that Christophe only moved here a few weeks ago, and that Em-J's mum works in the very place where the fire was.

They were surprised that I'm not actually in the band so I told them that I prefer being behind the scenes. And they gave me 'yeah, right,' looks, so fingers crossed Mum doesn't start making her famous phone calls.

Tonight, when I was watching them rehearse, I felt a bit sad and knew I would do anything to be in the band, but it's too late now. And I am happy to be included even this much.

I asked Em-J to ask Christophe to design the poster, and Em-J is going to find the equipment, the amps, mikes and mixing-board and all that. We also need to get a sound engineer for the night. I had no idea that there would be so much involved. I have to go to bed now so I don't doze off during the early rehearsal in the barn in the morning.

First, I am going to run down to the Hazel Wood and hang my sneakers on the note-leaving tree. If Christophe gets the idea he might decorate them for me, and if not I can say I was just mucking about and accidentally left them there. I kind of miss our Hazel Wood thing, it's like there are two totally different people, Christophe who's just a co-worker (and a slightly stuck-up one at that), and The Watcher who knows me and is there for me.

DAY THIRTY-NINE

It was *so* weird. We were all in the barn, the band rehearsing, me drawing a plan for where to put the stage, and Sammy-boy watching Beau in awe. Before we knew it, Mrs Granger from the Egg Farm was standing in the middle of the barn, yelling at us all to get out, and pointing her bony finger at me.

For ages we just gawped at her. My voice was shaking then as I shouted back that this barn was leased to my father until the end of this month, and that *she* was the one who had to go away. I was like,

'You have *no* right to be here!'

I can't believe it was me shouting that loud at someone.

Beau said, 'Yeah!' a lot, and started to calm Em-J down as she looked like she was about to throw something, or someone. Christophe ran over to where I was and in a softer voice than the rest of us, said to Mrs Granger,

'There's obviously been a misunderstanding, and we *will* be leaving the barn, either when Poppy's dad asks us to, or at the end of the month.'

As she started to walk towards him I was sure she was going to hit him, she's *that* unstable, but suddenly she went all jumpy-looking and starting telling *us* to calm down. Just as she got to the door, she said, in her version of an ordinary voice,

'There's *nothing* here that's yours, so don't you go nosing about!'

At the time we were all just weirded out by the whole thing, but thinking about it now, I wonder why she said that? I mean, there's nothing in the stone barn except my and Sammy's chairs from the greenhouse and three that Em-J brought over, and we already took out the buckets and the last of the hay after the audition. I swept it out myself and there was nothing to snoop after. At least that's what I thought until she said it, but now I'm not so sure.

And if there was nothing to be found, why was *she* there? What was she looking for?

I bet this has something to do with the food that's disappearing. Adam has Trug on guard duty outside most of the time and he hasn't barked or anything. But he's probably used to the Grangers. I bet it's them.

Adam says that they don't make much money from the Egg Farm because most people these days want free-range eggs where the chickens get to roam about, not the kind where the hens are all in rows in a shed, like on their place. I thought the Grangers must have been there forever but he told me they only moved in three years ago when Mr Granger's brother moved to the city to find easier work.

After lunch I phoned the place where Dad gets a lot of the farm equipment and they agreed to lend us a large wooden platform, four-feet-high and nine-feet-square, which will be perfect for a stage. In return we are going to let them put posters for their business around the walls of the barn.

I got a bit bogged down in all the organising, and so I just listened to the French stuff again for a while to get my mind off it. I am now imagining myself staging rock gigs in Paris so I'll need to get the next level of lessons because I only know the words for things like 'fish' and 'timetable' and 'excuse me,' but not for 'distortion peddle,' 'chick' or 'sound check.'

DAY FORTY

We all showed up at rehearsal with the same idea that there is something hidden in the barn, something valuable that the Grangers didn't want us to lay our hands on. Em-J was certain it must be jewels, Christophe reckoned old, gold coins, and Beau thought maybe a Viking's head. I hoped Beau was wrong as we got down on our hands and knees and up on chairs and searched every inch of the big, stone barn inside and out. After an hour we gave up and felt a bit silly.

Still, it is all a bit strange, Mrs Granger in the barn, and the stuff still disappearing from around the farm. Today some wool was missing from one of the sheep. It looks pretty funny now with a big bit hacked out of it. Dad isn't happy because in a couple of days when the shearers come he won't get a good price for that sheep's fleece.

Sammy-boy spent the morning pestering Christophe to bring him camping, and to stop him interrupting the rehearsal he agreed. Then Beau amazed us all by suggesting they camp just outside the stone barn to see if anyone comes there at after dark. So they are setting up the tent there tonight. At first Sammy was disappointed that his hero, Beau, wasn't included so now all three of them will be there. Em-J suggested that the next time we should *all* go. Now that would be wild, but I can't see her parents or mine agreeing to it. Or Christophe, come to that.

I spent the afternoon on the phone to get chairs. Most people will want to stand, but I think we need fifty chairs for around the sides. The hotel said they need theirs, but there's still a chance that the café might let us have twenty.

I didn't go to the evening rehearsal because I'm starting to feel like a bit of a spare. There's no reason for me to be there and I don't want the others to start to wonder why I'm hanging around instead of getting on with my production jobs.

I felt another twinge of 'left-outness' just now, but

pushed it away. I'm not letting myself feel bad any more.

LATER

Instead of getting sad, I wrote a song, my first proper one apart from the ones I would make up in the car when I was little and they'd last hours and be about the postman and the goldfish. This one is all about feeling locked into a different world from everyone else. It's called 'Whisper Me A Morning', and the chorus is about hearing someone from another world whispering secrets to me in the early morning as the sun rises and telling me that everything is going to be alright.

Although it was dark already, I just nipped down to the Hazel Wood and was disappointed to find my sneakers still hanging there, but as I got closer I realised that they were all decorated. I love them *so* much.

Even if I can't have Christophe, at least I can have The Watcher part of him.

DAY FORTY-ONE

I dressed up really rock-chick and wore my newly-pimped sneakers. The boys were just packing away the tent, and Em-J and I brought them over breakfast from our house. I thought I caught Christophe smiling when he saw me wearing the sneakers, but as usual we said nothing about it.

While we were setting up and the boys were demolishing the pile of cranberry muffins, Em-J said that this girl she knows called Barbara Montague phoned last night. I'm sure I went grey at the mention of her, because my hands started to sweat and my heart was thumping. She said,

'Barbara is getting back from her holidays just before the gig and wants to help out with singing some backing vocals, and maybe playing some percussion.'

I suddenly felt *really* angry – I'd done so much and here was Barbara thinking she could just waltz back here and be on stage in front of the audience that *I* will have spent hours getting in the door! I never felt so angry in my life as I did right then.

Just at that point, Beau and Christophe started agreeing that they really needed another backing singer and asked Em-J if Barbara was a good singer and how soon before the gig would she be back. That was it! It felt like a voice came from somewhere else, but it was really my voice, saying,

'ME! *I* can sing!'

Then they were all looking at me, and I knew I had to start singing right away or else I never would. The only song I could think of was 'Whisper Me A Morning', the one I wrote last night, so I closed my eyes to sing it, and when I opened them at the end of the song, the others were all just staring at me, smiling. Smiling in a cool way, not in a sympathetic way or the way you smile at babies or at bad jokes.

Then Em-J looked back at her notes and said,

'Thank God for that, I can't stand Barbara! OK, super-chick, you sing the lead on that one and we'll work out the chords and that tomorrow, and you can sing these two that Christophe finds it hard to do the vocal and play guitar on, and then you can sing this one instead of me because you are an angel and a star, and I'll teach you the backing vocals for the rest.'

The others nodded and that was it, that's how I got into the band. I think I caught them winking at each other but I can't be certain. Anyway, no one has mentioned Barbara since.

After the rehearsal Beau said,

'Great voice,' and Christophe even gave me a nod.

Then Em-J said to him,

'Hey, French boy, don't forget to bring spare strings tomorrow!'

'Are you French?' was what found its way out of my mouth.

Christophe looked puzzled and said,

'Yes, I know Hooper isn't a French name, but my dad's French and I grew up in Paris until I was eight. In fact I only learned to speak English after that.'

Which is the most he has said to me out loud ever.

It suddenly made sense, Christophe is the French for Christopher. I thought maybe he had just lopped off the 'r' like the way Emma-Jo became Em-J.

It's funny how all the interesting stuff happens just as you are going home and then you get to torture yourself thinking about it, and not about to find out what you want to know. I bet he still speaks French fluently.

I am trying really hard not to fancy him for three reasons:

1 Mindy is coming back and she'll want him.

2 All the girls will fall for him at the gig.

3 His mother told me he sees me as a sister.

4 He doesn't bother to look at me or talk to me.

5 I am tired of making a fool of myself.

6 Why would he go for me anyway, I never say anything funny like Em-J or Mindy?

OK, so that's actually six, but that goes to prove it even more.

They have agreed to lend me the chairs from the school thanks to Liza making a phone call for me. People are brilliant.

I *so* love that I am now singing in Farmer. I love it! I can't believe it!

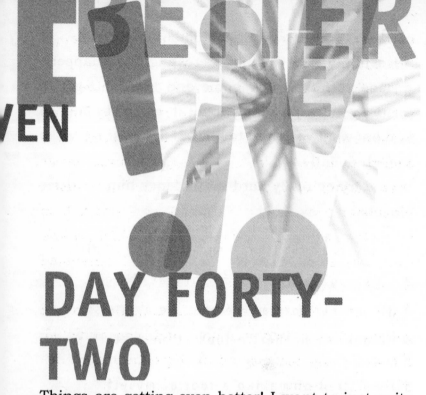

DAY FORTY-TWO

Things are getting even better! I want to just write about the adventure bit, but I'll tell the whole day just so I have all of it here in case I ever want to read back over and remember it in detail.

Everyone was really tired last night so we agreed to sleep in and not have a rehearsal until the evening. In the afternoon I sent the press releases and went into town to buy tape, string and pins for the posters, which Em-J says that Christophe says will be ready in a couple of days. Only TEN DAYS TO GO, which is good because it makes us work hard and it's not impossible. Also it means I don't have quite enough time to have a nervous breakdown.

Tonight's rehearsal dragged a bit, because we have to rearrange everything now that I'm singing. I'm not in the least bit shy about singing with them, which is a surprise, it feels so natural. Singing is much easier than talking! We know we're getting there, it's just a bit slow and you can't belt it out. We decided to take a break and went over to our kitchen which, thank God, was empty because they were all exhausted from the shearing day.

We sat in the little area in front of the kitchen garden with our food and juice, and I mentioned all the stuff going missing and the big clump taken out of the poor sheep.

Christophe then suddenly said,

'Oh my God! I can't believe I forgot this! And he almost choked in his hurry to tell us.

'When me, Beau and Sammy-boy were camping out the other night I was half-awake and half-asleep and heard people shuffling around. You know when you're really groggy and can't tell what's real or what isn't? Well, I heard a man saying something about "Looking harder", and "We've got to find them". I thought it was your dad or Adam, but now when I think about it, the voices don't match. Then I must have fallen asleep again, I was so tired. I *completely* forgot until just now!'

Beau couldn't believe that he had slept through it, but we could. (Beau is always the last to arrive at morning rehearsals.)

Em-J is action girl so she wanted to do something immediately. We agreed to finish our juice and sandwiches and then to go and snoop around the Egg Farm. All of us were convinced that the Grangers were up to something and that the answer to the stuff going missing must lie with them. The idea of going to the Egg Farm didn't really appeal to me, but when you're with a group of people, sometimes it's like they move into your head and you become more like them. That's why it's so important to have great friends, you don't want crappy people in your head or you end up doing crappy things!

And that's how we ended up in the lane going up to the Granger's house on the Egg Farm. It was still quite bright and I had no intention whatsoever of running into the Grangers and said so. More than once. Luckily Em-J was ready with a plan.

She said,

'OK troops, if Christophe and Poppy sneak around that big shed thing and try to see into the house, then I'll create a diversion.'

'What will I do?' asked Beau.

'You are the diversion I'm about to create,' she explained.

Before I could even think, Christophe had grabbed my hand and was leading me around the back of the chicken shed thing. That was the bit that totally scrambled my head. I mean. He doesn't even talk to me and then suddenly he's holding my hand!!??? I was so focused on having my hand held, there was no space left in my head to think about the fact that we were trespassing on the Egg Farm and might well get eaten alive by a Granger.

Then suddenly it was like he realised too, and quickly dropped my hand and hurried behind the shed. Crouched there we could hear nothing, so we inched closer to the edge and Christophe peered around the corner (with me still freaking in a good way about the hand-holding thing).

He went all serious and whispered,

'I can see them in their kitchen. The woman's cooking and the man's washing a cup. We need to get closer.'

'Won't they be able to see us?' I asked nervously.

'When our good and feisty leader gets the distraction together we can run for the boat they've stored right by the open window. It looks like we might be able to get under the tarpaulin.'

'Christophe, there's nothing bigger than a duck pond for miles. Why do they have a boat?'

'No idea.'

'What will we do once we get in the boat?'

'No idea.'

'Just so long as we're clear then.'

With that, we heard Em-J wailing and we both peeped around the corner this time.

Beau was half-carrying her and she was hopping along, leaning into him, pretending to cry really hard and clutching her leg.

Both of the Grangers ran out to the front of the house and we took our chance and ran over to the boat and climbed in, pulling the blue tarpaulin back over the top, covering us from sight. We could just about hear Beau asking the Grangers for a lift into town because his girlfriend had twisted her ankle. Mr Granger said they weren't a charity and shooed them away while Mrs Granger yelled after them that it was their own fault for not being at home where they should be. On the bright side, the Grangers don't have kids, but I do feel sorry for the chickens.

Christophe and I were sitting opposite each other on these wooden benches moulded into the boat, bent over so our heads wouldn't touch the tarpaulin and give us away. It was so dark under there that I could only just make out his face. I kept thinking about the fact that we had just had a real-live-actual conversation and that we were now stuck in a boat together in the dark.

For ages we could hear the Grangers complaining about Beau and Em-J, and young people, and all the people in the world. Then, for a while they were just talking about their dinner and the Egg Farm, and my back was getting sore so I carefully moved and sat on the floor of the boat. Christophe did the same and it meant that our faces were now only a few inches from each other and I could hear him breathing, but still couldn't see.

After ages and ages the Grangers started to say what we were there to hear. It went kind of like this –

Mr Granger: 'Do you think they know anything?'

Mrs Granger: 'How could they, they're kids. Not the brightest either.'

Mr Granger: 'They might have found the second set of papers, all that time they're spending in that barn.'

Mrs Granger: 'I'm starting to think there was only the one set, and we got them in the fire. I think we're safe and we're only getting ourselves into a flap looking for a second set that might not ever be found. It's years since your brother was told about them.'

Mr Granger: 'Maybe they're hidden somewhere else on that farm. Well, whatever happens, that soft city family won't get their hands on what should be ours!'

Christophe gripped my arm hard when they said that about the fire; did that mean *the Granger's* had started the town hall fire? But they could have killed people, why would they *do* that?

Christophe made a question mark on my leg with his finger and I leaned in closer and whispered back,

'I don't know.'

Then they were talking about food and prices of eggs and things for a few more minutes before Mr Granger went out to check the barns.

Christophe whispered,

'We should stay here for a while.'

I know being close together in the dark sounds all romantic (even if the guy isn't into you), but I was mostly worried that my stomach would start to make noises so soon after eating the sandwiches and I was dying to get out and back home. It was one of those times that seems better when you look back on it. Anyway, I now have to face the fact that I have a more massive crush on him than ever, and I have to work really hard at not making a fool of myself.

Just when I started to get used to being there, we heard more footsteps, but it was Beau and Em-J who lifted the tarpaulin cover and helped us out. We crept around the back of the chicken shed and then ran back across the road and past the stone barn all the way to my house.

We all agreed that it was obvious from what they said that the Grangers had started the fire in the town hall. I wanted to call the police, but Em-J pointed out that they'd find out that we'd been trespassing on the Grangers' land, and Christophe added that we had no proof yet. Beau was so furious that we had to stop him going back over, he looked like he might go for Mr Granger if he saw him again. We were just in shock.

While we waited for Em-J's dad to play chauffeur, we talked over all the angles for ages, then Christophe summed it up,

'OK, so there was two sets of papers, probably to do with this farm or the stone barn or something. The first set of papers got destroyed in the fire and the second set might be anywhere.'

We agreed that we don't have enough information to do anything about it, but we'll keep an eye out and maybe after the gig we can search the farm. It's not like they can do anything to the farm in the meantime.

All that excitement had me distracted from the fact

that I am going to have to sing in front of all those people and I don't think I can do it.

Only the idea that Barbara would take my place has stopped me from backing out.

HELP! I now know that the French for 'Help!' is '*Au Secour*'! And may I also add, '*Mon Dieu!*' and '*Merde!*'

It is good that Christophe and I now talk (even if he is not sitting up writing about *me* in a diary!) I am starting to think that maybe ... just maybe ...

Never mind.

DAY FORTY-THREE

I'm *SO* glad I didn't make a fool of myself by letting anyone know that I fancied Christophe. Today in the greenhouse, reading and chatting with Sammy-boy, he was telling me that his mum is feeling better these days and is playing chess with him in the evenings. He then said that he liked the camping with his brother and Beau, and that he wishes his brother didn't have a GIRLFRIEND, because that way he might be at home more.

I was really stunned and said,

'What's her name?' in a *way* too casual way that

would have been obvious to someone older.

He said it's Helen, and that Christophe was trying to keep her a secret, but that they spent loads of time together, and he'd do all these drawings for her all the time and get away from work early to see her.

And there I was getting excited about my two pictures when he was a veritable picture factory, churning them out for every female in the district no doubt! This Helen girl has probably been able to wallpaper her whole room with his stuff. I tried to keep my voice sounding like I didn't care and I said,

'Have you ever seen her?'

'No, but I know she's beautiful and she lives in town because he sometimes gets changed to go out there.'

I was thinking then that maybe she was just a friend, or that maybe Sammy-boy had it wrong, but tonight Christophe was half-an-hour late for rehearsal and avoided answering when Em-J asked him where he was.

Just when I think I can't be more of an idiot!

Well, anyway, I don't care. I even hate him now for lying to us. I am concentrating now on being an amazing singer, then I can show all of them, Barbara, the others at school, Matthew Blondel, Christophe, ALL OF THEM.

I was really focused at that rehearsal, which meant we did less mucking about and more work. Even if we had to perform tomorrow we could do a good enough job. I told Em-J I was really tired and she said that she and Beau would wait for a lift from her dad at the Hoopers. She wants to come over tomorrow to hang out, which will be nice. I'm not sure if I'll tell her about Christophe.

DAY FORTY-FOUR

I was in such a bad mood this morning when Em-J called over that she forced it out of me. I was lying on my bed and she was sitting cross-legged on the rocking chair. I was so pissed off that I put the pillow over my face and screamed into it and held it there. She laughed and said,

'Poppy, chick, you having a fit is more unexpected than Christophe not joking around or Beau being on time. So what's up?'

I just shook my head and she said,

'What's the point of going through something on

your own when you have a friend to talk to?'

When she said that, I took the pillow away from my face and stayed staring at the ceiling as I told her everything. About feeling like everyone else was better than me, about how (until her) I didn't have any real friends since moving here, and how nervous I was about the gig. It was so cool when she said,

'Well, there's no getting rid of me now, and I'd choose you over Barbara and her stuck-up bunch any day of the week. You rock, they just shop!'

She knew I was holding back and asked,

'And what about Christophe?'

'What about him?'

'Come on, chick, it doesn't take a genius to work out that there's something funny between you two. Do you hate each other or like each other?'

'I like him, he doesn't like me,' was how I summed it up, and then explained about what his mum said about seeing me as a sister, and about the fact that he has a girlfriend called Helen across town.

Em-J started to look concerned.

'Maybe they met at the end-of-term party that I met him at. I think it was a couple of days after the Hoopers moved here. Don't worry, chick, if you want him we'll get him for you!'

That's my worst nightmare, people doing things,

because it always gets mixed up. So I told her that I'd gone off him and not to do anything.

I know she didn't believe me, but she said,

'OK then, we'll just make him see that he made the wrong choice. I have a plan.'

I *love* Em-J's plans. This one involved us working out really cool moves, looks and steps that I can do during each song. The kitchen broom made a mike stand and a candle was the mike for the bits where I was moving around. We snuck into everyone's bedrooms and borrowed their mirrors, so we had this big bank of mirrors along the empty wall, which helped a lot. We agreed that while the boys are there I'll just sing as usual, and then on the night they will be as amazed as anyone.

Just as we had put the mirrors back and made ourselves some soup, the radio station called and wanted to interview us live by phone *that very minute*. We had no time to get nervous, and I spoke first about why we were holding the gig and then they asked Em-J about the band and she totally sold it as a great night out. I really talked and talked and didn't think anything of it. Maybe I just needed something good to talk about all this time.

I'm glad I told Em-J all that stuff, but also glad I didn't tell her about the Hazel Wood Girl and The

Watcher. I just really hope he didn't tell his girlfriend about it, I'd love to share this *one* thing just with him. I walked past the Hazel Wood later in the afternoon and could see a note hanging there for me, but I was too sad to go and look at it.

We didn't have a rehearsal tonight because Christophe said he had to work late for the farmer he works for. I bet he's not working that late, but he didn't think he could tell us he wanted to spend time with Helen instead of with the band.

At dinner we were talking about how to organise parking all the cars on the night of the gig, and Dad couldn't remember Beau's name and called him, 'Your relaxed friend', which made me wonder how people would describe me. I mean, Em-J is outrageous, Christophe is funny, Sammy-boy is thinky (oh, what's the word for that? I think 'contemplative' or something), Mindy is carefree, but what about me? I'm boring.

All my stuff goes on inside. I know that I'm way better than I was since the whole band thing started. I'd love people to think of me as creative and daring. Then when other people's dads couldn't think of my name they'd say,

'You know, that creative girl, the really daring one.' And they'd know it was me.

DAY
FORTY-FIVE

Mum wanted to call the police this time because all the goose eggs have gone, and all the raspberries and most of what was left of the broad beans. Dad calmed her down and promised to get a security camera. Adam didn't help by saying that they'd probably steal that too.

I phoned the music shop and they have only sold four tickets for the Farmer gig, so I am going to meet Em-J (who got the posters from Christophe at nine o'clock this morning) and Beau (who was supposed to get the posters from Christophe at eight o'clock this morning).

I'm still really hurt and pissed off that Christophe has a girlfriend and that he kept her a secret. I don't think I'd even admitted it to myself how hopeful I was getting. Now I just want to show him as well as all the others that I am worth paying attention to, that I am fantastic in some way. I can't leave the note hanging there any more. I'm going to go and see.

The note said,

Dear Hazel Wood Girl,

Your mission (as always, should you choose to accept it) is to let people know how you really feel.

From, Your Friend,

The Watcher

'Your *Friend*'!!! OK, well he couldn't make it any clearer than that could he?

I have to get ready now to walk into town.

LATER

It's so weird how everything can change so quickly. I felt *so* good yesterday with Em-J, and then I was pissed off at the note, and then soon after that I'm ready to forget the whole thing and lock myself away in my room for life and eat only bread. Mouldy bread at that. I hate my life. I keep getting happy for a while and then getting tricked by people only pretending to care about me.

I arranged to meet Em-J and Beau at four o'clock to do postering, but they didn't bother to show up, they just left the posters there with the manageress. There I was, like an absolute donkey, waiting outside the café with all these posters, until after half an hour I went in and had a cup of tea and was feeling really abandoned. It was worse then because Beau's mum came in to meet someone and as she passed me she said did I not go to the movie with the others. So I got stood up so they could go and enjoy themselves, and I suppose they thought I'd just go ahead and do all the postering work by myself.

Then, just when I thought things couldn't get any worse, I went into the music shop to give them a poster to put up by the counter, and there was Christophe looking at the guitar strings when he was supposed to be at work. I decided that I would win this time, and breezed over to the counter, gave Eddie (the owner) a couple of posters, and told him rehearsals were going great. By then Christophe had seen me and was walking over. There was another girl in the shop, but I couldn't tell if she was with him or not. And I was in NO mood to meet the famous Helen.

I put on a real cheery voice and said,

'Not helping with the posters then?'

And he said,

'I'd love to, but I have to get back to work in ten minutes. Would you like me to—', but I said,

'OK, see ya!' and bounced out of the shop and up the street.

I didn't stop to do any of the posters, but walked home by the double row of elms. It was the worst walk home I have ever had, even worse than all those times coming home from a hellish day at school. This time it was people I really thought were my friends who had let me down. I just cried all the way and was happy when it started to rain.

Luckily I had the posters in a waterproof bag, but I didn't even care about that.

Now I just think that Barbara and her friends must be right, there's something wrong with me, something that makes people want to walk all over me.

DAY
FORTY-SIX

I didn't have the heart to do the postering on my own this morning so I went into the greenhouse to read. Sammy-boy wasn't there and I just sat feeling sad and angry for an hour, not even looking at the French stuff.

Then Em-J comes walking up with a big grin on her face which made me REALLY angry.

'So super-chick, how did it go?' she smiled.

God, she didn't even say sorry! I started yelling at her. That's not my style and I was as surprised as she was.

'*How did it go? How did it go?* Well, Em-J, as far as getting stood up by your mates and waiting around for an hour and having to carry all the posters home by myself in the rain goes, it went *brilliantly*. And how was your afternoon with your boyfriend at the movies!?'

I didn't even wait for an answer, but ran out of the greenhouse and raced across the fields towards the Hazel Wood.

Em-J was going,

'Wait, Poppy, wait!'

So I shouted,

'I think I've done enough *waiting*, don't you?'

The next thing, I suddenly found myself lying in the mud with something around my knees.

Em-J had tackled me to the ground and wasn't letting me up until I listened.

She spoke really quickly.

'Christophe was supposed to be there too. I left him a message and his mum said he'd be finished by then. Our plan was to keep out of your way so that the two of you would spend time together without me and Beau, and that maybe Christophe would see the light, ditch his girlfriend and go out with *you*. *Love* the new temper by the way, every rock star should have one.'

There was about five seconds of silence, and I said, 'Oh!' and then we both started laughing.

She was really sorry, and had been so certain that Christophe was going to be there and that her plan would work and I'd be ecstatically happy. I could tell that she was really distressed that it had gone wrong, and she kept saying that she would never take me for granted like that.

Then I blurted out what else had been on my mind.

'Em-J, do you think I'm really boring compared to you and the others?'

'God no! I think that you say really good things while I just shoot my mouth off all over the place. We all talk about how kind and clever you are, and how smart and sophisticated you sound compared to us.'

'Oh,' was again as smart and sophisticated as I could manage in the moment.

We arranged to go and do the posters after the rehearsal (and after showering and changing). They had called a last-minute rehearsal that morning because Christophe got the morning off, but they couldn't get hold of me to tell me.

The others were waiting at the stone barn when Em-J and I walked in, covered in mud, although she was used to it, having been a member of the town's junior women's rugby team for the past two winters.

We were laughing and looking like we'd been sleeping rough for weeks.

'Don't ask,' Em-J warned the boys with a smile and a head shake. And they did as they were told.

The rehearsal was great, and every time I *almost* made one of the moves or gestures we had practised in my room, and then stopped myself, Em-J would turn away so we wouldn't crack each other up.

We found out that Christophe didn't get yesterday's postering message until late last night. Christophe wasn't as smiley as usual. He looks really tired these days. I forget sometimes that his mum is sick and that he has a lot on his plate. I have decided to act better towards him and be his friend. After rehearsals he gave a quick tired smile and ran off. I'm really confused as to how things got to feel so bad between us. I am sitting here on my bed at midnight, trying to work out how to answer his Watcher note.

***

I am going to write,

Dear Friend,

I don't know how to answer your note. My feelings are so all over the place these days that as soon as I show one emotion, it's moved on and has become something else. Sorry if I've been a bit weird.

From,

The Hazel Wood Girl

Should I just write, 'from' or make it, 'love from'?
God, I'm impossible!

DAY FORTY-SEVEN

I went down at midnight last night with a torch and thought I could feel someone near the Hazel Wood, by the ruined cottage. So I left the note and ran. It was probably just a fox.

This morning we rehearsed a new number where I do a duet with Christophe, which I know is just more scheming on Em-J's part. He looked a little sad again even though I could see his note from me sticking out of his back pocket.

Then a man came around from the local paper to interview us and take a picture. We all got ridiculously excited then and the mood really picked up. Remembering that we are doing it for Barry is really important so that we don't take ourselves too seriously.

Then tonight, me and Mum had just finished eating dinner (Dad and Adam were working late with the vet and the cattle) when there was a knock at the back door.

We expected it to be one of the men who help out on the farm, but this time it was Christophe, asking for me.

I didn't get *too* excited, but I was glad to have the chance to make things right.

He said he was wondering if I wanted to practice the vocals on the new number. I felt like saying something sarky like,

'Won't your girlfriend mind?', but instead I just smiled and said,

'I'll get my jacket.'

I started veering us toward the stone barn, even though I knew he was automatically headed for the Hazel Wood. I thought it would be less complicated that way.

I think that I was more relaxed with him now that I know that he's out-of-bounds (or 'girlfriended' as Em-J calls it). He was just like he is with the others, really funny, and even insisted on giving me a piggy back when I wasn't walking as fast as him. Then he threw me down onto one of the hay bales that we'd dumped outside the barn.

He was going,

'So, mademoiselle rock star, how do you mange to look so glamorous all the time?' and was shoving hay down my back and messing up my hair.

I was gasping for breath I was laughing so much.

As soon as he stopped I jumped up and grabbed a whole other bale and threw it on top of him and he pretended to be dying underneath it. We just messed around for ages, saying strange things in French (his French accent is *so* sexy), singing the songs in the styles of different singers and pushing each other off the hay-bale stage, and then we ran out of energy and stopped, and looked at each other.

'Hello, Hazel Wood Girl.'

'Hello, Watcher.'

'You can always talk to me you know.'

'I know.'

And then with the worst timing of anyone in the whole history of the universe, Mr Granger marched around the side of the barn. He walked off as soon as he saw us, but his being there was enough.

'Right,' Christophe jumped up, 'We're finding those papers.'

I think when we were interrupted it sort of reminded us that we don't usually carry on like that. We looked around the whole barn in case we missed something the last time, Christophe even climbed up into the rafters. They are definitely not there. Eventually, still a bit embarrassed about earlier, we decided to sing the new song, and practised it until Dad came in and said that Mindy was on the phone to Mum and wanted a word with me too.

Christophe asked about Mindy and I just laughed and said,

'You have plenty of time to find out how wonderful my sister is.'

He half-jokingly said,

'Well, if she's anything like you I like her already.'

That kind of made me feel good, and kind of made me nervous of when they do meet. I know I'll hardly get a look in with him once she's back, and fabulous Helen-the-girlfriend had better watch out too!

For now though, I am just loving the fact that we are now more friends than 'sort-ofs'. It's like The Watcher and The Hazel Wood Girl finally met tonight for the first time.

DAYS FORTY-EIGHT, FORTY-NINE & FIFTY

I haven't written in this for a couple of days because it's been all postering, rehearsing, getting the barn in order, getting the stage up ... all that good stuff. The school came good on the fifty chairs, which I collected with Adam and Liza last night. The local amateur theatrical society provided us with their lights; they really make the barn look like a professional venue. Dad is being really great and said that he'll take care of the electricity bill.

When I'm lying in bed about to fall asleep, I imagine myself singing in front of the audience and it makes me want to pretend to lose my voice so I won't have to do it. Then I remember that Barry Finch really *has* hurt his voice from the smoke and I know that I'm brave enough to do what I need to do.

The gig is TOMORROW and I just want it to be OVER!

Only ten tickets have been sold, but the others say that pretty much everyone just pays at the door. We've been rehearsing through the amps and with mikes so I've had time to get used to that. So I suppose there's nothing to be nervous of.

Nope. No good, I'm still sweating like a pig about it.

DAY
FIFTY-ONE

I was sick to my stomach all day. We had decided that last night was the last rehearsal apart from the sound-check. The extra equipment like the mixing board arrived at about two pm and Em-J and her techie friends Tank and Rainbow (really) had it sorted, so I went to run through all the lyrics and drink a carrot and celery juice to keep my energy up.

We had the sound-check at five and it all sounded really good.

At six Em-J and I went up to my room to change. We both looked fantastic, 'super-yummy', as she'd say. Em-J had on these white, loose jeans, a white sleeveless t-shirt, and a really old, light-green leather jacket. Her blonde hair was a little more spiked than usual. She added one long, dangly earring and a small diamond stud in the other ear, then finished it off with black nail polish on her short fingernails. I asked her about shoes and she said she wasn't going to wear any, and promptly painted her toenails black too.

Since my hair had gone so fair in the sun, I left it loose except for one small plait down the front on the right. I decided to wear the sneakers that The Watcher had decorated for me, and so had to build the rest of the outfit around that. I took out my dark jeans and Em-J said,

'No! We need you looking as cool as you sound, baby-doll,' and took over.

She decided on a short denim skirt with a bit of a flare, two belts criss-crossed over, long socks falling down, a thin jumper with a t-shirt over it (which sounds weird, but looks the absolute business). I would never have been able to think of how to put an outfit together like that. I *so* looked the part that I felt I was finally seeing who I want to be.

We checked ourselves in the full-length mirror and decided we were ready for the front cover of the coolest of music magazines.

One thing was really bothering me (there's always something with me!) so I shared it with Em-J.

'What if Barbara and her friends are there and start booing?'

'Not coming, chick. She's still on the island.'

'But you said she'd be back.'

'That was just to get you to sing.'

'Did my mum tell you I wanted to be in the band?'

'Your mum, your dad, Adam, and even Christophe. I almost had to hire a receptionist, I was getting so many phone calls about you!'

I suppose it's good when people get involved in your life.

The guys made such a fuss when we met them in the kitchen that I felt like the night was already a success. They especially loved the belts, and I caught Christophe checking out my legs!

Mum made us all eat spaghetti in veggie sauce, which annoyed me at the time, but later I knew she was right.

We advertised that it was starting at eight, but by eight o'clock there were only a few cars in the makeshift car park (aka the small fallow field). Em-J said that even if we only had ten people in the audience that we were to be really professional and play our best for them. I was a bit relieved that there would only be a few, but a bit sad too because it would mean we wouldn't make much money for Barry.

Then, by the time we had walked over, loads more cars, bikes and people on foot had arrived, and Beau said he counted eighty. Then in the half-hour before we went on stage, more people arrived, and Dad said we had over 250. I wished he hadn't told me that because then I went all shaky and was sure I'd be seeing the spaghetti again soon!

Next thing, Adam was up on stage and welcomed everyone, and rabbited on a bit about fire exits and stuff that I couldn't even understand because my heart was thumping inside my head, and my stomach was in my throat, and my feet and legs seemed to be gone completely. Christophe gave my hand a quick squeeze and his was as clammy as mine. I closed my eyes and imagined myself standing in the Hazel Wood, with a breeze blowing and the birds jumping about, and then I heard ...

'For the first time ever, put your hands together for ... FARMER!!'

The others bounded up onto the stage, Beau cracking his drumsticks together above his head, Em-J giving the crowd a thumbs up, and Christophe grinning and nodding and raring to go. I somehow got up there and looked out at the pool of people, all of them eagerly waiting to know what we were made of.

What was *I* made of?

I looked from one face to another, so many people from school who had laughed at me, ignored me, snubbed me. Then there were others, maybe people that I had ignored because I was feeling so sorry for myself. I knew in that moment what I had to do. No messing it up for the first few notes, no faltering before I found my feet. I glanced over to Beau, Em-J and finally Christophe, letting each of them know with a look that I was ready to sing, ready to finally be the person I was put here to be. I know that sounds dramatic, but I really felt it.

Em-J started with a slow riff, then Beau joined her with a steady hi-hat and soft snare. Then I could hear Christophe slide into the opening phrase and before I knew it, my voice was resonating through the speakers and throughout the stone barn. The audience came even more alive with each verse, each chorus, and with their cheers and applause at the end. We sounded amazing! My moves and gestures and little dancey bits went down well with the crowd, but even better with Beau who whooped at one hip move I made, and Christophe who yelled out,

'You move it, girl!'

Then it all became a blur as I grew stronger and more confident as one song followed another. Em-J and Christophe introduced all the numbers, until it came to the song I wrote that night not long ago, 'Whisper Me A Morning'.

I announced,

'This song is for anyone who has ever felt that they are alone. It's to let you know that you are always surrounded with people who want you to be happy and who want to share your life.'

People even applauded my intro! I sang that song as I have never sung in my whole life. I felt like everything that happened over the last year was leading up to that moment. The cheers were louder than ever and Christophe strode across the stage and kissed my cheek. As we kept playing, the audience moved in so close that the first six rows were squashed right up against the side of the stage, and the whole room seemed to be dancing.

Near the end, Christophe, while lining up the next song, said something really cool about a community not just being about old photos and documents, but that it was about creating new memories together, and you could tell everyone felt goosebumps all over.

When we reached the end of the set the crowd kept cheering for an encore. So we did the duet, even though we had decided that it might not be ready. It's kind of a love song, and I caught myself scanning the crowd for any girl that might be Christophe's girlfriend. There were so many likely candidates.

The applause and cheers went on for ages and my mouth was hurting from smiling so much. We all hugged each other and Em-J whispered to me,

'This is *one* of our dreams come true, supergirl, now we can get all the others in place.'

The yoga ladies had all brought brownies, mini-strawberry tarts, and all kinds of cakes and pastries, plus a huge vat of non-alco fruit punch for the younger people and a wine cooler for the adults. So the party carried on for two hours after we got off stage.

So many people were coming up and talking to me and I got to know about two dozen people who live in town and the farms around, who I didn't even know existed before. One or two people from school said they were sorry they didn't get to know me better during term time. Matthew Blondel from my class asked me to his party next week! At first I was going to say, 'I'll see', but I'm not that kind of person, so I thanked him very much instead.

Beau was mostly with his parents, aunty, uncle and cousins who looked so proud of him. Em-J was entertaining half the room with her stories, and I could tell that she was thinking how this was the first night of thousands like this, and that when she's famous she'll remember that tonight was when it all got started. We caught each other's eyes and winked.

I could see a whole crowd of girls around Christophe as he joked and hugged, and I just smiled, thinking about the notes and pictures from him that I'd be able to look at later on. I might not be his girlfriend, but I'm his friend and his fellow band member and that means a lot.

Sammy-boy was popular with all the younger kids because he was the only one who had a sibling in Farmer. Having a hedgehog probably helped too. He must have been tired because he went home early with Mrs Hooper.

Just before people started drifting back to their cars, my dad got up on stage and announced that we had raised the funds for Barry to be able to return to college. He then said that a private donor had added enough to buy Barry a scooter as a token of the town's thanks for his caring and bravery during the fire. I knew instantly that the donor was my dad, and

I felt really proud to be his daughter.

I so wish we had all grabbed a minute together before we left, but Beau was going off to a friend's house, and Em-J had to get a lift with her mum and dad. Christophe went at some stage too, but I didn't even get to say goodnight to him. I'm glad he didn't introduce me to Helen, that might have put a downer on a perfect night.

I still can't believe it, I'm a singer in a rock band and I just did my first gig and people loved it! Maybe those peanut-butter toast-sandwiches I'd eat on the way to school did have magical powers after all!

Mum just came up to wish me good night, which she hasn't done in years, as I usually go and find her downstairs and just tell her I'm off to bed. She told me that she was so happy that everyone got to see the girl that she always knew was special. I said,

'I wish Mindy had been here.'

And I meant it. Mum says it will be fun for us all to relive it, telling her about it when she gets back.

I can't sleep. It's a quarter to one and I'm wide awake. They'll have taken out all the equipment by now, but I want to stand in the barn and enjoy the feeling while it's still fresh.

DAY FIFTY-TWO

Of course, just when you think nothing more can happen... I was sneaking over to the barn last night around one am after failing to get to sleep, when I saw in the distance something moving near the Hazel Wood. I knew it must be Christophe because no one else apart from me goes there. More than anything on earth I needed to talk to him about the gig, so I ran across the cattle field in the pitch dark, stumbling every now and then. It was too dark to venture into the wood without getting whipped by branches, so I sat cross-legged just nearby. Some sounds vibrated a short way off, around the ruined cottage, which made me feel quite scared because it occurred to me that it might not be Christophe, it might be the Grangers, or worse.

Then my name was being spoken softly behind me.

'Poppy? Poppy is that you?'

'Who's there?'

'It's me.'

It *was* Christophe. He had a torch and I could tell he didn't have anything else in his hands.

'No note?' was all I could think to say.

'I just needed to be here. I figured ...'

And right then we both heard it clearly, a sound from the ruined cottage.

'Come on,' he said, and led the way.

I knew we just had to find out who it was, and what was going on. It sounded as if things were being moved around inside, dragged from here to there. 'Bodies!' was my first thought, and not a helpful one. I've never been inside because of all the warnings we'd been given about the walls collapsing.

Christophe took a deep breath and we walked inside, and then he shouted in a slightly wobbly voice, 'Who's in here?'

For a moment his light searched around, hitting only bits of wall and floor, and then it landed on a person, perhaps the last person we expected to find.

Sammy-boy.

We just stood there looking at Sammy-boy who was sitting on the ground with his mouth open, shaking all over, and not able to speak. Around him were piles of old eggs, vegetables, unripe grain, and rotting raspberries sitting on little beds of unprocessed wool. Nothing mattered suddenly, no details or questions, and I went over, sat beside him and put my arms around him. He started crying then and couldn't stop, so I just kept hugging him and telling him that it was OK, that no one was angry with him. When he could talk he said,

'But now I have to go to prison,' and started crying even harder.

I thought I would break from it.

'No, no, you're staying right here with us.'

With that, Christophe, who had been just standing there, picked up his little brother sat with him on his knee on a low piece of wall. Sammy-boy seemed even smaller than usual. Christophe gently asked him,

'Tell me what this is about Sammy-boy. That's it. I've got you.'

He said it in a broken mixed-up way and with loads of sobs between the words, but we finally understood that Sammy-boy heard their mum on the phone to their dad one night soon after they had moved here. She was sounding upset and asking,

'And how are we supposed to pay for food and basics this winter?'

Frightened that there was no money and they'd all starve after the summer was over, Sammy-boy then started to save small bits of food from his meals, like apples and cereal bars, and hide them under his bed. Eventually he got too hungry to keep that up, and began to sneak out really early in the mornings or last thing at night and take things from our farm. He said because we were kind. Soon there was so much stuff under his bed that he had to find another hiding place and knew that no one came near this old cottage. During this last week he started to get really worried because the food started to go rotten and he couldn't sleep at all at night for worrying about it.

Sammy-boy was crying in little whimpers by now and said,

'What are we going to do to eat this winter? If Mum's hungry she'll have to go to hospital again.'

I could hear a catch in Christophe's throat as he said,

'We will always have enough, Sammy-boy, always. Mum just wanted to make Dad think a bit more about the money he sends us, that's all, it's all sorted. And I have a Saturday job once school starts again. And it's OK, but you have to understand that Mum will be going into hospital every now and again, and then she'll be out after a while like always. I promise you never have to worry about anything. I'm in charge.'

Then Sammy-boy looked over at me and said,

'Poppy looks after me when you're not there.'

'I know,' he said, 'we're really lucky to have her.'

That made me feel sad, but also it made me feel good, like I make a difference. Most of my life I've felt as if I'm in the way or not as good as Mindy, and that things would be better if I wasn't around. Now I feel that I do matter. When I go back to school I'll remember that, and even if Barbara and her lovely bunch go back to making fun of me, and even if people steal my lunch (not that they'd get away with it now!), at least I'll know that I make a difference to one little boy.

Christophe said we should all go home to bed, and he made me take the torch so I could see my way, and he carried his little brother home in the darkness.

When I woke up this morning I felt happy about the gig and also really sad to think that a teenager has to feel like he's in charge of his whole family.

Liza stayed over and it feels like she's always been here. At breakfast I told Mum, Dad, Adam and Liza about what happened in the ruined cottage. Liza and Mum had tears rolling down their faces and that set me off too. None of them are even a tiny bit annoyed with Sammy-boy, they just feel really bad that he had all that going on inside his poor little head.

Dad got really furious, which is not like him at all, and started pacing up and down the kitchen. I think he was angry that he didn't work it out, or didn't help the Hoopers more. He kept saying,

'I'll sort this out, I'll think of something.'

Christophe arrived right after that and asked to speak to my dad, who took him straight through to the living room. I ran up to Mindy's room, which is just above the living room, and put my ear to the floor. I heard enough to understand that he was trying to pay Dad for the stuff Sammy-boy hid in the cottage, but Dad wouldn't have it and was telling Christophe not to worry and all kinds of good things that made the tears start rolling down my face again.

Mum came in just now and told me that we are having the Hoopers over for dinner, so I have to hurry to help Liza get the chairs back to the school.

DAY FIFTY-THREE

Last night was another one to remember. I think I need a day off from amazing things! When the Hoopers arrived for dinner, Sammy-boy said sorry for taking the stuff and we all hugged him and told him that we love him. He had a box under his arm and looked at his brother, as if to ask what to do next.

Christophe said that they had a bit of an announcement to make, so we all sat around the kitchen table. The Hoopers had spent the afternoon clearing out the rotting food from the ruined cottage, and while they were doing one last check, Christophe found this old tin wedged at the bottom of what would have been the old fireplace. At first he thought that Sammy-boy had put it there and opened it up expecting to find carrots or beans inside. That's when he found a bundle of papers wrapped in plastic, and instantly wondered if they might be the second set of papers that the Grangers were talking about.

Back at home, Mrs Hooper and Christophe read through them, and it seems that they *are* all about the stone barn. They say that the stone barn belongs to *this* farm and always did. And there's more. There were also papers proving that the Egg Farm was sold to Adam's dad just before he died. That means that the Egg Farm belongs to Adam and not to the Grangers after all.

We couldn't believe what we were hearing and we made Mum read the documents there and then. Being all lawyer-y, she doesn't get overly excited, but she did say that it seems to be true and they will need to get it all verified.

Adam was dazed. He said that he'd love the chance to turn the Egg Farm into a real chicken ranch where birds can roam and scratch about in the sun and rain.

'But what about your teaching job in the far east?' I asked.

'Well, I'd already decided not to take that job,' and he squeezed Liza's hand, 'but I'll still be going there in late October for a couple of weeks ... on our honeymoon.'

That was just *way* too much new stuff, *way* too quickly, and we all sat there trying to work out what he said. Then Sammy-boy saw the ring on Liza's finger and told her it was a very nice ring, very big (and it is!). Then there were hugs and kisses all round and Mrs Hooper, Liza, Mum and me were crying with being so happy, and the guys all laughed at us. Then Mum and Mrs Hooper had a million questions for them about the wedding and when did they know, and all that.

Good thing I was there to finish the cooking and serve up, otherwise everyone would have starved and not even noticed. We all talked and talked about the Egg Farm, the Grangers, the engagement, the gig, over and over until it was really late. I don't even think about talking or not talking any more, I just do it as much as anyone.

This afternoon the police confronted the Grangers with paperwork and told them that the place doesn't belong to them. Of course they already knew that and were livid that the evidence had been found. Mrs Granger then went on a rant, spitting that they should have burned down all the farms, not just the town hall. Which is how the police discovered that the fire had been started by them. Mum said that they will need more proof like fingerprints or confessions if they are to put the Grangers in prison for it, but at least they'll be out of everyone's way for now. Within two hours, they'd packed up the basics and fled. They left the boat (which is, of course, an important landmark on the 'fancying Christophe Hooper' trail).

We all trooped over to help tend to the chickens; they were in an awful state. Mr Granger hadn't cleaned the sheds out properly in years. Dad even let me put on a mask and gloves too, and had me collecting the fresh eggs. Some dead birds were left in their stalls, which was the saddest thing, but Dad dealt with them first.

Adam explained to me that even when he has the new open runs built, many of the chickens will just stay motionless in one place, that it's hard for them to change from the way they have lived for so long. I know what he means, but I hope that one day, if they really want to, they can do things differently. I hope that even chickens can change.

After dinner we had a meeting of all band members at Em-J's house.

We laughed like crazy people, and demolished the best part of a giant pizza, going over every tiny moment of the gig, what everyone did, felt, saw, heard. When you're in the band you notice and care about little details that other people would find boring.

We also talked to Barry Finch on speaker phone. He's out of hospital and thrilled about the money and the scooter. He claims to be the biggest Farmer fan in the world and will be there in the front row for the first gig after he's fully recovered.

Liza and Adam have asked us to play a few numbers at their wedding reception, and the café have told us we can play every Friday night as long as we give them a cut of the profits. Em-J has already got calls from people saying they are starting their own bands, so hopefully they can come and play at our nights in the café, which we are calling The Harvest Nights.

Christophe and I sat beside each other on the couch all evening, and at one point he started playing with the zip on the corner of my jacket. Em-J noticed and immediately started teasing him saying,

'So Mr Guitar Man, what would Helen think of you

snuggled up so cozy beside another girl?'

He looked confused and said,

'I don't know anyone called Helen.'

Which made me really confused too. Within a minute Em-J was grilling him alone in the kitchen under the guise of having him help bring in mugs of peppermint tea. She phoned me once I got home and reported that Christophe doesn't have a girlfriend and hasn't had since he got here, so we have no clue what Sammy-boy was on about. That time he was late for rehearsal was because he had to fix a mistake that another farmhand had made.

Now I am combing over everything that has happened in the last couple of weeks and rethinking it with this new information. I still can't work out if he is into me or if he's just being his usual friendly self. Guys are lucky, their heads work in straight lines like tractors while mine dances about in every direction.

DAY
FIFTY-FOUR

Over breakfast Adam told me he has great plans for the Egg Farm, which he's now calling the Egg Ranch because it will be so different. He doesn't like doing any of the business side of things, and jokingly asked if me and Em-J wouldn't mind leaving school and coming to work for him. Sammy-boy, who had just shown up, said,

'My mum was a business lady before,' and then toast got in the way of him saying any more. It was enough though, and Adam went off to make a call.

I decided to find out about this 'Helen' girl that

Sammy-boy said was going out with Christophe.

Through more mouthfuls of toast, he thought for a second before saying,

'No, not Helen, uuummmm ... Hazel, yes,' he giggled with his secret, 'He writes her love letters and leaves them on a tree, and sometimes he's happy when he comes in and sometimes he isn't happy and he says, "Girls! They are *such* a mystery!" like this ...', he rolled his eyes and grinned in a perfect imitation of his brother.

I realised then that Sammy-boy must have seen some of his notes to me, or mine to him, and doesn't know that I am the Hazel Wood Girl. It still doesn't mean that Christophe actually likes me, but hey, it's a start. I can't believe how ridiculously relieved I am that he isn't 'girlfriended' after all.

I just chilled out in my room all day, and at dinner Adam said that Mrs Hooper is going to run the business side of the new Egg Ranch, which should mean plenty more money for the Hoopers. She has been feeling so much better since they moved here and even if she has to take some time off, there are loads of people around to help out.

It's now about eight-thirty at night and I'm off on a mission to the old Egg Farm to check there are no cats, canaries or other animals that need looking after, ones that we missed when we saw to the chickens.

LATER

I just got back, and ended up with *SO* much more than the one-eyed, mangy old Golden Labrador that's probably lying at the end of Sammy-boy Hooper's bed right now.

The dog was filthy and cowering in the kitchen of the Egg Farm, and not until I'd fed him would he come to me. I looped my belt around his collar and was leading him out down the lane and across by the stone barn when I noticed Christophe and Sammy-boy walking towards me. Probably because I knew that he *might* like me and didn't have a girlfriend, I felt really nervous, as bad as that day in the supermarket when he was looking at bread.

'Hey, what are you up to?' Christophe grinned and Sammy-boy looked from one of us to the other like he was working something out.

'Just rescued this poor old soldier. I don't suppose anyone wants a slightly yellow dog?'

'Yes, me! Me! I want a yellow dog!' Sammy-boy jumped up and down and started giving me a list of all the reasons he should have a dog, with gestures to demonstrate. It was great to see him so happy and excited and I kept pretending I was unconvinced, which made him even more determined. My personal favourite (with actions) was,

'And, and, and, I can chop down a little tree and throw it for him to catch, and then make him eat a ham sandwich, like that.'

When he got to,

'No, because, Poppy, I can run really fast like vvvhhuuum!, and he can run with me and be my friend, and I'm the boss and I'll tell him not to step on the hedgehog.'

I handed him over, and Sammy-boy darted off with the dog to ask his mum if it was alright. I could never say no, and I don't think his mum will either.

Christophe yelled after,

'Bath, Sammy-boy! You *and* the dog.'

That left me and the guy I was by now madly *insane* over, standing there in silence without a dog to pretend to talk about.

We sort of both looked at the ground for a few seconds and then Christophe said,

'Look ...' before pausing and then starting again.

'I was just about to leave a note in the Hazel Wood,' he said, holding a piece of paper in his hand.

'What does it say?' I asked, with a straight face at first, but then I couldn't help starting to smile.

He crumpled it up and stuffed it into his back pocket, took a deep breath, a really deep breath and launched into,

'It says—

Dear Poppy,

I know I have really messed things up, right from the start. But I hope you can forgive me and not just think of me as some idiot who isn't worth your while talking to. I really fancy you, and would like you to be my girlfriend. Am I being a complete prune or do you fancy me too?'

'Who's it from?' I smiled, faking an innocent look.

He didn't reply, instead he playfully picked me up and carried me over to the barn wall and kissed me and kissed me. They were kisses that I couldn't have dreamed of, they felt that good. I still can't believe it.

Yup, just checked my head again, still can't believe it.

Later, I retrieved the original note from his back pocket and it actually said,

Dear Hazel Wood Girl,

Thank you for being such an angel.

Love from The Watcher

I've kept it and put it up beside the bunch of flowers picture and the cartoon of me.

Then we went to sit on the hay-bales and I had to know why he had ignored me for so long, and not wanted to talk me. I was totally floored when he said that he was just too nervous and shy, and that he thought I wouldn't want to have anything to do with him when the others were around, because he knew I was such a sophisticated city girl. It just goes to show how we can all really mess things up just by thinking! Also he was feeling really bad about moving here and thought that I was already in with people like Beau and Em-J and that I thought he was just an outsider. The laughing at me was from nerves, and he thought that *he* came across as an idiot in the supermarket and at the fish barbecue.

Anyway, I soon told him my half of things and we spent the next couple of hours talking and kissing and singing, before he walked me back here and quickly kissed me again before running off home across the field. I could hear him shout, 'Yes!' in the darkness which was *so* lovely.

I can't take it in (did I mention that yet?). I never thought this would happen. I wonder why there's no word that means the exact opposite of lonely? Whatever it is, that's how I feel now, like the spaces are all filled up. I looked at his pictures until my eyes were too heavy.

DAY
FIFTY-FIVE

Mindy came home this morning, and we caught up with what we'd been up to for the past few weeks (except about Christophe). For the first time I wasn't just listening while she gabbed on, and it meant that sometimes we talked over each other, but she listened a bit too. After a while she laughed and said,

'So you've learned to talk then!'

That would have bothered me before, I would have thought she was criticising me, but this time I just said,

'Yes, and in French too.'

She couldn't believe it and after my little

demonstration, said that I probably learned more French than she did. I can tell that she will make room for me now, I just need to insist more. I need to let her know that she can't walk all over me like before.

I was a bit nervous (well actually, sick with nerves) that she would flirt with Christophe and he'd fall for her, but they met this lunchtime in our kitchen when he dropped in, and afterwards she dismissed him, saying he's too 'nice' for her, that she likes mean'n'moody older guys. He didn't seem that interested in her either and spent most of their conversation telling her about what a good singer I am. It's funny how you can worry yourself half to death about something and then it doesn't even happen.

I'm glad she's back and already I feel much stronger around her, like she can't take the shine off me. We hung out in the greenhouse for a while and she said that she might move some of her stuff in, take down the kids' pictures and have friends around. I said firmly, but not in a mean way,

'No Mindy, not possible. This place belongs to me and Sammy-boy. You're welcome to visit, but you'll have to find your own den.'

I was expecting a huge fight, but was amazed when

she just shrugged and said, 'Whatever, it's not that great anyway.'

Then, very Mindy-style, she talked for an hour about these two boys that she couldn't choose between, before heading off into town, surprised at the big hug I gave her as she left.

DAY FIFTY-SIX

Yesterday Christophe and I met up in the Hazel Wood and walked all around the whole district. He showed me the farm where he works, and I recognised most of the people from when they were at the gig.

Later, in the café, we got seriously mushy, staring into each others' eyes over cold cups of tea. He told me that hazel were his favourite colour eyes. I guess that's the colour they are, a real colour after all. But it didn't stay romantic for long as loads of people kept coming over and telling us how great the gig was, and one guy asked could he buy a Farmer t-shirt. Christophe said they'd be for sale at the next gig.

Right now at this moment, Christophe, Em-J,

Beau, Sammy-boy and I are all lying or sitting in the summer cattle-field, the end that looks toward the Hazel Wood. And I can just make out the shape of a note, waiting there for me.

The cows are way up the other end of the field and have taken all the flies with them.

We finished a game of rounders a while ago, stopping only when the chair-leg bat broke in two. Now Beau is asleep, Sammy-boy is wrestling with Mr Puddles (that's what he called his nervy new dog after one too many accidents on the kitchen floor), Christophe is sketching the new Farmer t-shirt design, Em-J is flicking through a magazine and chipping her black nail polish with her teeth, and I'm writing this. When they realised it's a journal, Christophe got all excited and asked,

'Am I in in it? Can I read it?'

'Yes, you're in it. You even have a bit of a starring role,' I teased him, 'And no, you can't read it.'

'That's right, super-chick,' Em-J said, 'Keep your mystery.'

'Yes, we girls are *such* a mystery,' I smiled, as Christophe looked at me sideways.

I'm really looking forward to the next few weeks, getting ready for the Harvest Nights at the café with Farmer. It's funny that I'm really not worried about school, because I know things will be really different. It's a shame that Christophe and Sammy-boy will be at Em-J's school, but it's not like they'll be a million miles away.

Mum has allowed me to take charge of the geese and I'm selling the eggs to a deli in town. By the autumn my hazel trees will have a harvest of hazelnuts which, if the squirrels and birds don't get them first, the deli will sell for me too. We are all saving up so that a year from now Farmer can play a gig in Paris, first stop on Em-J's well-scrawled paper napkin. Mrs Hooper and Liza are going to help us out with organising that, and we'll all stay with Christophe's dad.

I know that all sorts can happen between now and then, that down things will follow up things, and around it will go once again. But these days I can open my mouth and talk out whatever's going on inside, even sing it if the mood should take me.

'All good, super-chick?' asks Em-J.

All good. Because now, I have friends.

Plenty.

It's official.

Hope you enjoyed Poppy's story,
now meet Tia in *Blue Lavender Girl*

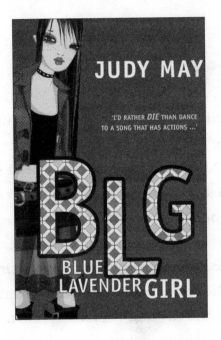

DAY 6

This morning the post arrived after Mum and Dad had left for work. I read my end-of-year report and binned it. I know they won't ask. I used to get really good grades, As and Bs, and now I do really badly. I just can't be bothered. Anyway, don't need to think about it for another six months at least.

Parent-teacher meetings are in the bag. When my folks get the letter from the school asking why they weren't there, I say that I *definitely* told them about it last week. They know they forget about a lot of things when it comes to me and they feel guilty. They say they'll call in and talk to my teachers at some other time, but they never do (luckily for me!)

I think they peaked with my brother Aidan, I'm like

that second Mars Bar when you are full from the first one – OK, but not really worth it.

LATER

Mum and Dad have either

a) found my report in the bin

b) had a phone call

c) heard something on the radio about teenagers

d) decided my frozen pizza pockets for dinner were so bad that I must be evil ...

Or anyway something has made them feel like making a decision about me.

Now I have three days to come up with a 'constructive and educational' plan for the summer or I am being sent to Aunt Maisie's for six weeks.

Aunt Maisie is a proper aunt, she buys me things, leaves me alone when I need it, doesn't ask awkward questions, talks to me, doesn't boss me about ... did I mention she buys me things?

She is more fun than the rest of us put together and being with her instead of Mum and Dad would be bliss. BUT I couldn't stand to live in the countryside.

Mum says it's not the middle of nowhere (but it is) and that there is plenty to do. There is plenty to do if you are a granny, not if you are a teenager. I do not consider making rag dolls from old socks to be a 'fun activity', even if I did love it when I was seven. Anyway, it doesn't matter, I'm not going. I'm off to talk to Kira's mum, she's a genius at coming up with stuff to get me and Dee off the hook with our folks.

DAY 7

FACT: I am now just about angry enough to do something reckless, but too angry to think what that might be. If not even Kira's mum is on my side, then it's safe to say that everyone is against me.

Kira was sitting there too and we were all drinking chamomile tea because they had just read up about it. While Kira's mum said, 'Tia, I think it would be a really good idea for you to get away for a while,' Kira was nodding like she was the wise woman of the west or whatever.

Then they both started this double-attack about me not being happy. Well, show me anyone who is happy! They are not even happy, they've just got more feel-good sayings and CDs than the rest of us.

Really.

I called Dee and said that if I can get out of this Aunt Maisie plan then we can both go into town this weekend and hang out at the market stalls and see if we can pretend we are sixteen and get jobs. She said that she was hanging out with Timmy this weekend, except that it took her half an hour to say it because she kept going on about all the cool things he said about her.

I called Aidan and he was out.

INTERESTING INFO: If you get my dad away from my mum you can sometimes encourage him to have an independent thought. But the plan was bigger than the both of us and he said that he and Mum would visit every second weekend, which for some bizarre reason was supposed to make me feel better.

no one wants me here.

Well FINE!

I will probably be dead in two days anyway from having eaten nothing but cornflakes. I even had to make milk out of yogurt and water tonight, which doesn't really work.

DAY 8

I'm glad I didn't waste brain cells thinking of anything else to do for the summer, because I just found out that I'm going to Aunt Maisie's anyway. She always comes here so I've never seen her place. Mum tells me it's a large cottage in its own grounds, but if she thinks that will change me into one of those *Pride and Prejudice* girls she's very much mistaken.

I'm sort of relieved though, because I hate everyone right now, but I won't let them know that.

I need to use every minute I have to make it so they won't go into my room while I'm away. That way they can't pull another stunt like the salmon-coloured, flowered wallpaper that appeared when I was off on the weekend school trip to that farm. I am going to push all the mess near the door so it's impossible to get through.

I put all my favourite clothes into a big suitcase and then took them all out again deciding to wash everything first in case she doesn't have a washing machine. I know she will, I just ... God, I don't know.

I went around to meet Kira and Dee at the burger place, but they sounded worse than my mother. They kept saying that I'd have a good time and they wish they were going and that I might find a boyfriend there. I told them I don't want a boyfriend, but I didn't say that I didn't want to be all ridiculous like they are over the Timmys. The other guy's name is not actually Timmy I just can't be bothered learning any more names of guys they like, so from now on they are all just Timmy. Once we are all ancient and they get to the altar, then I'll learn the guys' real names.

I didn't even get to say goodbye properly because Dee's brother's friends arrived in, and this needed the girls' full attention in case things don't work out with the current round of Timmys.

I had to ask Dad for money and he said 'How much?' That bugs me because he should really have thought of it and then he should have given me more than I asked for just to make sure I was OK. Instead he gave me exactly what I said and counted it out really carefully like it was a million.

Mum put her head around the door to say goodbye. Then said she had to give me a hug as she wouldn't be seeing me for a couple of weeks, and gave me one of her hugs where there is enough room for two extra people between us, so it's really just her hands on my shoulders and bending a bit to the left.

Trundle used to snuggle up to me and nuzzle my hair with his nose. Aidan gives these big bear hugs, but only when he is coming or going for ages, or on special occasions. He still hasn't called back, which makes me feel like I've lost my only real parent.

I looked up at the sky and wondered what's happened to the stars these days. There are never any when I think to look up. When I was really little and we spent time in Dad's uncle's place by the beach, there were loads of stars. We used to all lie on the beach and Dad would teach us the names of the stars and Mum would get them all muddled up and not on purpose. It was such a laugh, but I haven't explained it very well. It was one of those 'you-had-to-have-been-there' things.

I nearly forgot to pack this diary, good thing it was on top of my jeans with the beads otherwise I would have left it behind. It's weird that I have written more in this than in English class for the last year.

***

I am in bed early.

PRETEND REASON: To get enough sleep to be up bright and early to get to the train in time.

REAL REASON: I am so angry with them that I keep wanting to bite someone's head off whenever either of them says anything, and I don't want to fall out with them just before I go or they might never let me come home.

Blue Lavender Girl by Judy May
Available in all good bookshops

Blue Lavender Girl by Judy May, 2006

ISBN: 978-0-86278-991-6

Now meet Tammy in *Copper Girl*

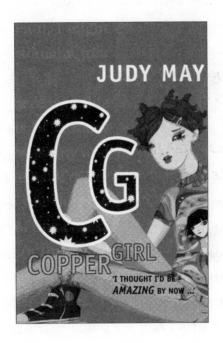

JUNE 12

I woke up at 6 am because I forgot to close the curtains last night and the sun came streaming in. I decided to wear my blue t-shirt with my faded jeans and my Converse. I did my hair in a couple of little pigtails to try and make it look like something other than just long and straight.

I spent half an hour writing to Charlie and Hellie and then read a book for a while. It's really cool, all about a girl my age who speaks lots of languages and gets to help foil an international smuggling ring. Next year I will pay more attention in German class now that I have a reason! I wonder if you can do espionage as a degree? I guess they'd have to call it something else, so no one would know. I'll ask Dad if I can learn to ski too, but that would involve money so I know he'll say no. I sometimes fantasise that I'm older and can ski and ride horses and ice-skate and play tennis, and all Adie's lot and the Rat Pack are trying to be my friends. Ridiculous, I know, but I can't help it.

Dad asked me to mind the shop again so he could take Mum and Mikey to the doctors for Mikey's check-up. He can't walk properly because his feet are a bit funny, and so they need to get it sorted. He's so cute though with his tufty, auburn baby-hair and the way he laughs all the time as he waddles around. He's the only person in the world I get hugs from these days.

Mum won't let me wear any of what she calls my 'weird stuff' when I'm working. As *if* people would change their minds about wanting a carton of milk and a newspaper just because I'm wearing a shirt with a Japanese cartoon and have three earrings in each ear. I don't mind looking after the shop, I just hate the way they *tell* me rather than ask me, and the way it's always so last minute. Like as if I don't have my own life. Actually, now that the girls are gone, I don't, but they still shouldn't presume.

Then when they got back from the doctor's I

thought I could do something like go to the library and that's when Dad handed me a *huge* bag of dry cleaning to bring up to the laundry place. It's half a mile away and I don't have a bike or anything, and as I took the bag Dad said something about my face, about my having an attitude. God, I hate him. I know for a fact that he spent every summer as a teenager swimming, fishing, rock-climbing and playing golf with homemade golf clubs with Uncle Paul. I might ask him to tell me that story again later tonight, just to remind him.

On my way back from the cleaners there was this old lady who was struggling with loads of laundry bags so I asked her if I could help. She was tiny and smiley and had white hair tied up on the back of her head with a purple gem clasp. She was well dressed for an old lady; you know the way some of them dress for comfort or as if they are still in the era they liked best, well she looked really classic and she didn't have a million Kleenexes hanging out her sleeve.

Luckily she only lived nearby because those bags weighed a *ton*, it was like she had just got her armchairs dry cleaned or something! Mrs Miggs (weird name, I know) invited me in for a cup of tea. I actually really needed it at this stage, and plus, I was in no mood to go home, so I said yes. She had all these pictures of horses everywhere, and her house smelled of lavender, but not in a spray air-freshener way. (Our house always smells of rice for some reason.) When I asked her about the horses she told me this really cool story about how she got her first horse when she was seventeen. First we had to pour the tea as Mrs Miggs said,

'You need tea to oil a good tale.'

She had been helping her mother wash the front step and polish the door when a beautiful chestnut horse just arrived, trotting along with its saddle half hanging off. She ran after the horse and tried to catch it; it was running so fast that it took her a while to notice this young man who was running behind, all irate looking. So, by now she'd caught the horse by the bridle, and the man thanked her and asked her to help him to get the horse back to his father's stables, because he'd hurt his leg in the fall. Her mother looked at her disapprovingly (I know that look so well!), but she went anyway. When they got to the stables, the young man's father started to yell at them both for the state of his magnificent horse. The young man explained to his father that he had to borrow the carriage horse because his own horse was too afraid of the trains to make the trip across the tracks and over to the sports ground. His father yelled at him even more and told him that he had exactly one day to find a new home for that useless old nag who cost him a fortune in oats and hay.

The young man had nowhere to put his own nervous grey horse and so she (young Mrs Miggs) said he could keep it in her back garden while his father calmed down. She spent the summer meeting up with the young man in the lane and sneaking into the garden to feed the horse and ride it before her parents woke up; they were fine about the horse, not so fine about the man.

I was so into the story that I was surprised to see someone else in the room.

'Has Granny been telling you her "horse and hand" story?' This really tall girl, about my age, with black hair in a shoulder-length bob, went over and gave Mrs Miggs a hug and then gave out to her for fetching the laundry bags. Mrs Miggs explained that I had helped and the girl grinned at me. She had the most teeth I had ever seen in one person, a bit like a horse herself, but good looking. She smelled like a farm, but not the worst bits of a farm.

'I heard about the horse, but not about a hand,' I said. I hate how I always blush in front of new people, but no one noticed, or at least they didn't say anything.

'Well, by the end of the summer my grandad had

asked for Granny's hand in marriage,' the girl said as she poured herself a cup and reached for a slice of cake, 'That's why we call it the "horse and hand" story.'

She then looked me up and down and said that she loved my style, and Mrs Miggs said, 'Yes, indeed, very unique.'

I felt my face burning so I mumbled that I had to be back home and they both said to drop in anytime.

I think I look ordinary, even though I wear arty clothes. I bet people can tell that I'm ordinary, all dressed up with no place to go, and all that. I don't care, I like my clothes, and my friends think I look good too. It's only Adie and Doris who ask me if I made that outfit myself, but they are professional bitches and it's their job.

Sometimes when I look at Adie sneering at me, I can't believe that we used to be best friends. We met when we were four at our first day at kindergarten and she used to be round at my house all the time – until we were nine and Doris joined the school and took Adie out on her dad's boat and then that was it. I remember Mum kept asking where Adie was and I couldn't think what to say, and then she eventually stopped asking. It was another year before I became friends with Charlie and Hellie and I can't *believe* that Adie let me sit on my own at lunch (or with other groups of friends who would be a bit confused as to why I was sitting with them) for all that time. She didn't start to get really, really horrible until I had new friends, but we decided early on not to stoop to their level although we are just as bitchy behind their backs, which means I'm not as brilliant as I pretend to be.

The whole thing is really stupid and it means I sometimes can't get to talk to Johnny Saunders because I don't want her to see me talk to him because she and Doris would tell him horrible things about me. One time after I got an A for an English essay and they got Ds and the teacher had me read it out at assembly, they told everyone that I had a verruca on my foot and that's why they couldn't invite me to their pool party.

That girl at Mrs Miggs's looked amazing, not pretty and over-groomed like Adie and Doris, but like she could be a model when she's older, really different ...

Copper Girl by Judy May
Available in all good bookshops

Copper Girl by Judy May, 2006

ISBN:978-0-86278-990-9